The Desert Island Game

Cat Voleur

SLASHIC HORROR
PRESS

Other titles by Cat Voleur

Revenge Arc
Puppet Shark: The Novelization

Kill Your Darlings

The characters and events in this book are fictitious. Any similarity to real persons, living or dead, is coincidental and not intended by the author.

Originally published in Australia by Slashic Horror Press in 2024.

ISBN-13: 978-0-6457638-6-7
Cover design by Wayne Fenlon
Interior design by David-Jack Fletcher
Edited by David-Jack Fletcher

This page left intentionally blank

To all the lovers, past and future, who I would not want to be stuck on an island with.

This page left intentionally blank

Part 1

1.

The best sex is the kind you get at the end of the world,
but you can only ever get it once.
Then, the world is over.

2.

"Did we miss it?"

"I guess so." Bea's words were slurred as she answered.

She'd felt sober enough when she'd been sitting on her own, looking at the blazing orange of the sky above, but even that short sentence was hard to string together. Was it the massive amount of alcohol in her system? Or was she experiencing some sort of shock?

"Huh." Evian plopped down beside her lover on the warm sand.

Huh indeed.

The situation was beyond strange, and Bea found Evian's casual attitude toward the whole affair only increased her own anxiety. The frustration roiled inside her as she forced her eyes away from the inferno.

The blonde beside her was gorgeous. Obnoxiously so. She was so relaxed that it might well have been any ordinary day for her. The fiery clouds cast a warm light over her long, smooth legs as she stretched them out toward the water. She reclined onto her elbows in a way that arched her back, pushing her breasts toward the heavens. Heavy makeup from the night before smudged beneath her eyes for a perfect dramatic look, which she made sure to show off when she brought a hand up to push the long hair from her face. Bea swore she moved in slow motion. Even without the cameras, she was posing for a fucking photo shoot. The whole thing was very apocalypse-chic.

Bea had longed for an eternity to be this close to her, but now she found she couldn't look even a second longer.

Huh.

"Is that all you have to say?" Bea snapped.

The end times were not the sort of thing you should be able to miss. Not something to be slept through. Most certainly, they were not something to wake up from.

"What do you want me to say?"

"Something," Bea pleaded.

Evian sighed, but it was not enough of a pause to let her pretend she was thinking of something good. Then she was speaking, her lips glistening and her tone unconcerned. "I think it's cool we're both still here."

"Cool?"

Bea was at a loss.

"Yeah. Right?"

"Everything is gone, Evian. Everything—everyone— we ever knew. They're all just…gone. And you think it's cool?"

She wanted to cry. She couldn't fathom loss on such a scale as she was now experiencing. Couldn't even begin to name the people she'd lost and would miss, the people… All those people.

Still, Evian didn't look bothered.

"I mean, I wish they weren't gone. But I didn't want to die with them." When she looked over and saw the incredulity on Bea's face, one of her perfect eyebrows quirked up. "Did you?"

Of course, she hadn't.

Bea had finally gotten everything she ever wanted, and the woman of her dreams to share it with. For the first time in her living memory, she felt she had something worth holding onto. Yet she couldn't imagine being so callous about the cost.

She choked on her reply.

Last night they'd shared everything. Champagne. A bed. One another's bodies. Bea had let go of herself, all her secrets, all her insecurities, every inhibition she'd ever held. Evian had been there every step of the way, opening up and treating her to the sweetest pleasures she'd ever known. After years of longing, the two had intertwined their desires into a reality of unmatched bliss. They'd been operating as a single person by the end.

Now, the women seemed little more than two strangers on the beach.

Bea was barely able to turn her head away before the champagne and bile came up to leave a dark stain on the white sand.

3.

The hangover was bad.

It was vomiting up black goo every fifteen minutes and flashing back to her twenty-first birthday bad. Nothing made sense.

One moment Bea was in a strange bed, and flames consumed the island around her. The next, she was in her dorm, curled up on the bathroom floor as she listened to her sister laughing and mocking her from the other room, certain she was dying.

Evian Lemaire was dabbing sweat off her forehead, and they were in a place she didn't recognize.

There were disjointed memories from what she thought was the night before.

She was at a bar, coughing and spluttering between

shots.

She was on a beach house, stripping off her T-shirt.

She was shaking her head over a bright-pink cocktail begging her sister. "No more. Please no more."

A soft hand was trailing bruises up her inner thigh.

They were all happening at once.

A phone rang somewhere in the back of her mind—her mother calling to yell at her.

But Bea couldn't know that.

It hadn't happened yet.

"What have you done to her, Beatrice?" she would ask once Bea answered. "She's just a child. What have you done?"

Her sister was dead.

"Drink! Drink! Drink! Drink!" They chanted at the crowded happy hour.

Her mother was dead.

Bea was bound to the headboard by her wrists, and Evian Fucking Lemaire was holding a glass to her lips. "Drink."

So she did.

The water was sweeter than all else, and Bea drank so deeply of it that she forgot to breathe. Only when it was emptied did she find herself collapsing back into the bed.

When she landed, it was in her first apartment, and she had just received the news. She had stopped trying to make sense of where—or when—she was. Whatever was going on could just get on with it, for all she was concerned. She was too exhausted to fight, or even to try to understand.

Giving up wasn't the end of the world. She seemed to recall that had already happened.

4.

D amn tomorrows.
Bea's mouth was dry and bitter as she drank greedily from the glass on the bedside table. The cool water had nothing to do but slosh around inside her empty stomach.

She had a vague recollection of what had transpired before her nightmare had scrambled all the pieces of her past together. It didn't seem real, but neither did it seem as important as it had the last time she'd been awake.

All that mattered to her was getting some food so she could gulp down more water without the risk of puking it back up.

She was shaky on her feet as she got up from the bed. The silk sheets clung to her sweaty form and threatened to suck her back down to the mattress before she could escape their pull. The ceaseless spinning of her little world threatened to knock her right back down on her ass with each step.

She closed her eyes until the sensation passed. Only then did she stumble to the door, her footsteps careful and really fucking loud in her throbbing ears.

It had been dark and humid in the bedroom, not to mention coated in the sweet stench of her sickness. The hallway was different; clean and bright and comforting.

How could the sky possibly be burning when everything inside was so beautiful?

With more confidence in her heart than in her uneasy steps, Bea teetered to the kitchen.

"You feeling any better?" Evian greeted her from the far side of the marble counter.

Something looked different.

She had gotten cleaned up and gone with a softer make-up look that matched her tight jeans and loose knit, crop-top sweater. The casual attire was rare for her, but stylish enough that it wasn't out of character. There was something wrong, but it wasn't the clothes.

Evian was sitting straight on her stool, having selected the side of the counter that faced the kitchen, and therefore, faced Bea. The blinds of the windows behind her had been drawn, blocking off what would have otherwise been ample natural lighting. The overhead alternatives cast a cool glow over them.

With Bea's limited brain capacity, it seemed normal.

Well, someone's version of normal.

For Bea, the word had different connotations. It was something more akin to a pull-out couch, a residual scent of insecticides, and the sounds of neighbors bickering through the paper-thin walls of her apartment.

It made Bea's head fuzzy to try and recall any of those things. That had been another lifetime; best left in the past with the rest of her nightmares. It felt impossible, a place and time she no longer belonged in.

Neither did she fit in here—as if her sickness hadn't been evidence of that.

The beach house was commercially immaculate, made with the sort of over-the-top minimalism deemed desirable by the ultra-wealthy. Bea had seen several such impractical locations used as sets when Evian was filming. It looked, still, as if there would be a crew of people ready to preserve the illusion of such effortless opulence in such an impractical location. The expensive hardwood floors looked pristine and polished, with no sign of sand being tracked through. The warm, reddish hue perfectly matched the specks in the marble, and the lacquered blinds that stopped any sign of the outside world from infiltrating the kitchen.

As she braced herself in the wide, white arch of the hallway that looked out into the kitchen, Bea couldn't understand how she, of all people, was living there. She couldn't quite understand how she was living at all.

"Bea?"

She realized she hadn't answered Evian's question, which had been asked in lieu of a warmer, more personal greeting. Like the one you'd expect from a lover. The pain in her head was not as bad as it could have been, considering, but it was heavy with fog and impossible to direct. She almost couldn't remember what the question had been.

You feeling any better?

Am I?

"A little." Her voice was not her own. The sound poured out like the croak of a frog, deep and gravelly.

Evian nodded to a glass sitting in front of her, half-filled with sparkling water. Bea needed no further invitation to claim the drink for herself. The carbonation scratched the itch at the back of her throat, even as her stomach protested to the addition.

"That was pretty gross," Evian told her. No doubt she was referring to the hours spent vomiting up her guts.

"Sorry," Bea answered, sitting down the empty glass.

She sat down herself as well, before she could succumb to the feeling she might do more of the thing for which she now offered meek apologies.

At least her voice sounded more recognizable after the beverage.

"I thought maybe you were possessed or something."

Like all of Evian's comments, this one was glib. It was smooth and cool, and it rolled off her tongue in a way that implied it couldn't matter.

Nothing mattered.

"Is that why you left me?"

The question hadn't meant to sound so accusatory, but it did. Evian didn't seem to care much one way or the other.

"You just wanted to sleep after that first day. You kept calling me Elle."

Bea's vision flickered at the name. She felt lightheaded, and could see the outline of the bar again, where her underage sister had chanted and hooted until they had both been over-served. The image faded as Evian continued speaking, the real world coming back into focus.

"I figured I'd leave, and let you get some rest."

She sat there, numb, waiting for the words to finally catch up to her.

"After the first... How long have I been out?"

"This is the third morning."

Two days.

She had been sleeping for two days.

Bea was glad she was already sitting down when she got the news, because it made her knees buckle. Part of her wanted to fall. She felt so weak.

"I'm sorry." She didn't know what else to say.

Evian shrugged. "Me too, I guess. You told me you

were a lightweight. I just didn't think it would be this bad."

She shook her head—a motion she instantly regretted. Her headache, which had been little more than a dull pressure, exploded. Her vision filled with white spots. There were little men with jackhammers doing demolition work inside her brain.

It must have looked as painful as it felt, because Evian got to her feet across from her. "Can I get you something to eat?"

She meant to refuse, but her stomach answered for her. The rumble tore through her abdomen at the mere mention of food.

"Toast?" Evian pressed.

"Yes, please."

What was presented to her a few short minutes later was not just toast. It was nothing short of a miracle. The crispy, buttery bread was warm and delicious. It helped absorb some of the mess she'd made of her insides. But having Evian bring her food? That was unimaginable.

In the time she'd worked for the woman, Bea had never seen the model get anything—not for herself, let alone for another person. She was always surrounded by staff and coordinators and agents who could hand her whatever she wanted. Water. Trendy coffees. Sugar-free gum.

The only time Bea had really seen Evian do anything was for the cameras, and she was the sort of person who would only give one take.

It hit her then.

That was what was wrong with her partner's appearance.

There was not a single camera on her.

No phones, no tablets, no crew, no adoring public.

It truly was just the two of them. With the threat of the end no longer looming over their heads, that reality was sinking in. This was uncharted, unexpected territory. It proved to be more intimate than even the things she had let Evian do to her when she thought there'd be no tomorrow. That had been just the two of them as well, but still performative in its own right; a final show of indulgence.

This, however, was real.

Bea finished her toast, and reached for the bottle to refill her glass. She downed that in one, long drink, pleased to find that it settled better. That fact gave her the courage to speak again, something Evian seemed to be waiting for.

"I'm really sorry you had to see me like that."

"You've seen me in worse states."

That was true enough. She had only worked for Evian for about a year before things had gone to shit, but a person couldn't work for her long without seeing some things.

"I suppose I have."

"It was scary at first, though."

Bea looked up, surprised by the uncharacteristic vulnerability of the admission "Scary?"

Evian gave the smallest shrug of her shoulders, as if to brush off the emotion. "I didn't know if you were going to be okay."

"I am."

"I know. But I didn't know what I'd do if you weren't."

Bea felt something rise in her throat other than bile. A lump. "I didn't mean to scare you."

Evian opened her mouth, and hesitated. "Bea…"

"Yes?"

There was a terrible storm of a secret brewing in those lovely eyes that she was on the precipice of sharing. Bad news, certainly. Bea wasn't ready for that. She would break. She felt the cold coils of fear winding their way around her heart as she held her breath, gripping tighter with each second of silence.

The harder it was for the blonde to speak, the more fear settled between them.

What had she learned while Bea slept? What hell had she gone through alone while Bea had been so selfish as to abandon her to solitude in the aftermath?

She didn't want to know, and yet she could no longer take the suspense. "Evian?"

She smiled. In the blink of an eye, whatever troubles she'd been lost to were gone, and her face lit up the room around her once again. "Come sit with me?"

Bea didn't point out that they were already sitting.

Her cloudy mind dared not think any longer about what had just happened, or what terrible axe might hang just above her head.

Evian took her hand to pull her away from the kitchen counter, and where Evian went, Bea was sure to follow.

The trip wasn't far, and with each step threatening to make her head spin, Bea was grateful when it ended. Evian took her just from the counter, around the half-wall divider to the living room, which was only about a dozen steps courtesy of the open floor plan.

The couch where the couple settled sat facing an empty wall. Almost empty. There was a clock near the corner that read 11:49. The rest of the wall was a blank slate, devoid of color. It looked so different than the peachy pink it had presented as when they first arrived. Now the blinds were drawn, and there was no color from the window to reflect.

She had not noticed just how stark the room seemed until now, but even that feeling of clinical discomfort was fading as Evian pulled her into her arms. Everything felt better there. The world became timeless, and Bea was able to doze in and out peacefully, like the bad things outside were nothing but nightmares.

They sat like that a long time, Bea in and out of wakefulness. She felt almost healed by the time she spoke. "Evian?"

"Yeah?"

"Thank you for taking care of me today."

Evian twisted her head some to look down at her, a gentle smile on her lips and an affectionate look in her grey-green eyes. She was still gorgeous, she couldn't help it. It was a softer beauty, though, the kind that made her look almost maternal.

"We have to look out for each other, right? Now that it's just the two of us."

Bea nodded, and the motion of her head no longer pained her. She wished their closeness could last for eternity.

"Can I tell you something?"

"You can tell me anything." Evian stroked her hair.

"You've surprised me."

"Because I brought you here?"

"That too." Bea craned her neck to look at her more. Even from this angle, she was perfect. "You could have brought anyone, you know. Anyone would have considered themselves lucky to come here and see the end of the world with you. Anyone could have come, and they would have died happy."

"But we didn't die."

"And I never would have expected everything else from you. Everything, since we've been here."

Evian smirked, and didn't pull her hand away for another pat. She let it keep wandering instead, through the choppy ends of Bea's short hair, down her neck, her fingers tickling some at her spine. "Is that so?"

"I didn't mean it like that," Bea whispered, even as a

blush crept into her cheeks. "I just never saw you as the sort of person who would…" she trailed off. Her brain was still fuzzier than she realized. There were no adequate words to describe what she meant.

"You didn't think I'd take care of you?"

Evian didn't sound offended or surprised.

"Or be this soft," Bea admitted. "This is a side of you I've never seen."

"Not many people have."

"You always just seemed so…"

"So what?"

"In control?"

Evian's fingers had stopped moving, but she pressed closer, cupping the small of Bea's back. "Having control means being responsible for the people that serve you."

There was something so final about the way she said it.

"It does?"

"Yes. Otherwise, you won't be able to hold onto the power you have. You've seen how demanding I can be."

"I have."

"Would you have pushed yourself so hard if I wasn't also looking out for you? If I weren't paying you on time, and giving you bonuses, and bringing you along on all those fancy trips?"

"I suppose not," Bea said.

Only after she said it did she realize it was a lie.

It had never been about the money or the tech or the working vacations to beautiful parts of the world that would have been inaccessible otherwise. It had been a chance to be a part of something larger than herself; a part of Evian. Proximity to her had been payment enough.

She seemed to know it, too. Her sly smile widened.

"Well, you're different. Most people wouldn't give me their all just because they had a crush."

Bea felt the warmth in her face crawling deeper and more rampant in her skin. It was silly to think that after all they had shared, it would still be so humiliating to own her attraction. Somehow it was worse than expected to be exposed in such a way.

"How long did you know?"

"I've known for a long time."

That should have been no great surprise. She was Evian Lemaire. She was the most beautiful, successful, self-made woman in the country. She was probably used to everyone being head-over-heels for her.

Still… "You never said anything."

"We were working together. I didn't want to embarrass you. Or complicate things."

So she should be embarrassed. A pathetic, school-girl crush on someone that saw her only as an employee. A computer geek. Her greatest fear realized.

"What changed?"

"When we knew the end was coming anyway, what did it matter?"

It was not the most encouraging answer. Bea rolled onto her back proper, so she could look up at Evian more squarely. "Why me?"

"Why not you?"

Bea figured the question was rhetorical, but she had an answer. She had several answers. This conversation about the island had brought all her old fears bubbling back to the surface. She felt much larger all of a sudden, large enough to crush Evian's delicate lap with her head.

"Why not you?" Evian repeated slower when she saw the look on Bea's face.

"Because..."

But she couldn't say it.

"Don't make me ask a third time."

Evian's voice had a familiar edge to it, not dissimilar to the tone she employed at work when it was time to command a room to her bidding. Yet this was lower in her throat and left not the slightest space for hesitation.

"I'm fat," Bea answered, the words a shameful whisper.

Before she said it, she'd wanted to cry, but no sooner were the words out of her mouth than she was laughing. Her embarrassment dissipated, a remnant of the world before it burned. It felt ridiculous to care about such things under the current circumstances. Last month if she'd been told she'd be living rent-free on an island with nothing to do all day, her first resolution would have been to lose the weight.

But as she sat in total comfort, being caressed by a goddess of a woman, it didn't feel like it mattered. It felt like the funniest joke a person could tell.

"I'm fat," she repeated. "And I'm not pretty enough to be a plus one to the end of the world."

How utterly absurd.

She laughed until she was breathless, her lungs burning and her abs sore from contracting so much. Evian let her work it out before she spoke again. "I'm glad you hear how silly it sounds."

"It does, doesn't it?"

"It does. But Bea?"

"Yes?" She rubbed some of the tears that still lingered in her eyes.

"If you ever say that you aren't pretty again, I'll have to punish you."

Bea's laughter died.

Evian's voice was soft, but serious. There was no sign she was joking.

"Punish me... like that night?"

"Yes. Did you enjoy it?"

Bea nodded.

It was difficult, if not impossible, for her to think about that night they'd shared. It was a memory so perfect as to be inaccessible, like calling upon such secrets would burst through the bubble of time that had captured them. Details or not, she felt how her body heated at the mere mention.

"Yes. But...it scared me, too."

"Scared you how?"

"It didn't feel real. Nothing did. It still doesn't. Even now, when I try to think about it, I can't. I'm scared that if we do that again, I might lose touch with reality altogether."

"Would that be so bad?"

Maybe not.

Her hangover was doing the heavy lifting in compartmentalization, but Bea knew that wouldn't last forever. Tomorrow had come, with another one on its heels. Reality would become little more than mourning soon; struggle and strife and hard questions. How would they make it home? What would be left for them? Who would be left? How long could they make it?

Eventually she'd return to being her worried, normal self, with problems that were not so easy to laugh away.

The fantasy was better than that. But it wasn't real. She couldn't entertain such a thing until she was certain she could make it back to the real world—what was left of it—after. That she would not drown in the delights.

"I'm not sure I'm ready for that."

Evian looked down at her in understanding. "You don't have to be ready. Not yet."

Bea shuddered.

It felt inevitable to her then, that she would succumb. If Evian wanted her in that way, Bea knew she wanted it twice as bad.

But the fears, now that she remembered them, proved harder to silence.

"How will we survive?" she whispered. "What are we going to do?"

"Shhh," Evian said, and stroked her hair again. "Don't worry. I'm going to take care of you."

5.

Bea had not slipped back into the feverish phantoms she'd experienced nights prior—not once she was cleaned up and brought back into her lover's embrace. But even restful sleep could not chase away all that the two would have to deal with.

The couple had been prepared for a wild week, and had packed well for it. But they were now halfway into their second week, and Bea worried about how dire the situation must be getting.

Evian had been the one to make all the arrangements.

Bea didn't know how much food or clean water they had. She didn't know if there were backup generators, or what would be required to run them. If they were already on emergency energy, which seemed likely, they would need to cut back on their comforts, and be more strategic.

The more the thoughts raged, the worse her guilt grew.

For two days she had left Evian to deal with these terrifying concepts alone while Bea had slumbered off her over-indulgence. The knowledge weighed heavily on her chest—that she hadn't been present, let alone helpful. It was worse knowing she'd need to be brought up to speed before any true semblance of peace could be found.

Looking at Evian was the only thing that could calm her nerves while Bea waited for her to wake.

She was beautiful while she slept.

Of course, she was beautiful while she did anything. She had the sort of face that could change with ease, could be fierce or soft or vapid, but never ugly. She looked all the more stunning now that Bea was beginning to see there was a woman of substance beneath all her beauty, someone with wisdom and empathy.

How had I never seen that before?

How could she ever have thought of this woman as fragile? As spoiled? As naive?

Evian had proven on two occasions now that she was deeper than Bea could have ever known. She had more worldly knowledge too. It was something she hoped Evian would share with her, would teach her, if they could live long enough to share such fortune again.

How could she bring up such a serious topic though?

How bad would the assessment be?

Bea had not forgotten about the ominous look of foreboding that had overtaken her lover the day before, still unexplained.

It was far easier to concern herself with the beauty beside her. The honey gold of her soft hair. The creamy pink of her lips. The way her long lashes fluttered with just the faintest—

"Stop staring at me." Her voice was whiny with exhaustion, and she gave the command without opening her eyes.

"I wasn't staring."

"You were. You are."

"You're just so beautiful when you sleep."

"I'm beautiful all the time."

Evian had never been one for false modesty. Another woman might have been put off or envious, but Bea found herself more enraptured than ever in the raw confidence.

"I just wanted to take a minute to appreciate waking up next to you. Before things get serious."

Evian's eyes were wide open and shining at the word. "Serious?"

"Not with us." Bea corrected. She couldn't contemplate having that conversation just yet, and could not risk getting distracted. Anxiety over their situation had eaten at her long enough. With her head cleared and the sense she now had something to lose, she couldn't let their survival sit on the back burner any longer.

"Oh." Evian did little to hide her disappointment. Bea swelled some to know that Evian wanted such a talk. That she was interested in more. "What did you mean, then?"

Bea fought the urge to please her at all costs, and found it was more difficult than she'd ever realized. She wanted to please Evian, right down to her core, whatever it took… But the coming conversation needed to be had, even if her lips were so full and glistening and—

She pressed forward.

"We have to talk about serious stuff. Food and water. The electricity is probably going to go off soon, and I don't know how to set up a generator, if we even have one. I don't know how to operate a boat. I don't know how we'll get back."

"Oh," Evian said again. She closed her eyes once more and snuggled back into the covers. "Don't worry about that."

Alarm bells went off in Bea's brain. The guilt she'd felt about leaving Evian alone for two days to consider such terrible logistics was fast giving way to panic at the notion they hadn't been considered at all. Perhaps they had both been in a state of denial.

"I am worried about it."

"Bea—"

"And it's not like we can just have supplies shipped in if we run out. We don't know if there are supplies. Or anyone left to deliver them. If we survived, maybe there are others, but as long as we're on this island we'll never know. In the meantime, we'll need to figure out food. I can't hunt, and I don't know what sort of animals live on the island. I haven't even seen any animals on the island! There's a good chance they'll be as desperate for food as we are, and if they get aggressive—"

"There are no animals on the island."

This was not entirely a relief, as far as their food supply was concerned.

"Fish, then? Can you fish? I went once, but I wasn't very good. And we don't know if the fish are even safe to eat." Panic gripped her, those alarm bells ringing louder and louder. "Fuck, we don't even know if the water is safe."

Evian started laughing.

Bea couldn't speak for a moment, stunned by the sound. When she did, it was with irritation. "I'm not kidding."

"I know. I just think you're cute when you're worried."

"Evian, this is serious. This is our lives." We could die, is the part she didn't say. She hoped she didn't have to, but was increasingly sure she'd have to work up the nerve to do so.

"Bea, I told you I'd take care of you."

"Yes, but—"

"Do you trust me?"

Do I?

It was a hard thing, bouncing back and forth between her conflicting visions of Evian as strongly capable and fiercely inept.

"Bea?"

She bit her lip. With all the implied insults she'd accidentally tossed Evian's way the day before, she still hadn't seen her lover look so wounded until now.

"I want to," she said. "I do, I just…"

"You don't think I'll be able to protect you?" Her beautiful face stayed expressionless.

"I know you'll try." Bea thought back to the toast Evian had made her, and how grateful she'd been. She thought about how safe she'd felt sleeping in her arms just a few hours earlier. She longed for a time when the simple gestures would have been more than enough. "But I also know we're in a lot of trouble right now. I don't want you to bear the burden of all that alone."

"It's no burden."

Evian settled herself back into the blankets, like the discussion was over. Bea could not help but play with her side of the fabric in her restless fingers.

That was the problem.

It should be a burden. Evian should be worried, especially if she's planning to take responsibility for our future. Bea didn't want to hurt her any further with the reminder that she was losing control—especially when they had lost so much.

"I just don't want to let this be a problem."

"Then quit making it a problem." Evian's tone was dangerously close to a demand as she sat upright again and met Bea's gaze.

She tried to approach it from a different angle. "I know you don't want me to be worried. But I'm a problem solver, you know this."

"I know, but there's no problem," Evian insisted.

"I'd just feel a lot better if we could talk it through."

Evian sighed, looking away, conceding some ground.

"Please?"

"Bea..."

"I'll have an easier time relaxing when I know beyond a shadow of a doubt that you and I are going to be okay."

"Fine. But if we have to have this talk, can we at least do it after breakfast?"

It felt like walking into a trap to agree to such a thing. If Bea's concerns had any merit, food rationing may soon be on the table. But she had at least convinced Evian to talk, and agreed that the conversation may go better on a full stomach. It would also give her the opportunity to see how they were doing on food. To see the damage for herself.

"Sure. I'll go make us something."

One meal, she hoped, would not be the difference between life or death. She realized, rather quickly, it may not come down to that.

Upon opening the fridge, she discovered it was almost overstocked. There were four full cartons of eggs, little green baskets of organic berries, tubs of yogurts, cartons of orange juice. A peek into one of the drawers confirmed they were brimming with food as well.

She couldn't remember them being so well-prepared during their end-of-days celebration. She knew they had eaten well, but couldn't remember the details as to what. The only specific libation she remembered was the alcohol.

She turned around to see the chilled, glass drink case opposite the fridge was still fully stocked as well, with sparkling and non-sparkling waters. There were bowls of fruit out, and boxes of granola, and some of her personal favorite pre-packaged snacks. These were all things she had not taken note of until this very moment.

Starvation was still a real threat, being as isolated as they were, but it would not be imminent. It seemed more likely that the fresh food would go bad before they had a chance to eat it all. That would come with its own problems, but Bea took some comfort in it as she set about cooking breakfast. She put water on the stove for tea, and dug around to see if there were grounds for the coffee maker.

She found them a little too easily, nearly a year's supply, in the first drawer she checked.

Finding her paranoia was only rising, she finished setting up the coffee with one of the bottles of water—just in case what came out of the faucet was irradiated.

Evian came down in jean shorts and an oversized T-shirt that slipped down one shoulder to reveal a neon green bikini string that tied around her neck. Her makeup was perfect, and there was a small tugging of Bea's heartstrings, to know that Evian had made herself up for her.

It is for me, right?

There was no one else.

It was one thing she was grateful for about the apocalypse. It had cured her of many esteem issues. The Bea of last month would never have believed such an improbable thing as Evian putting on makeup with her in mind.

Evian finished her tea herself, steeping it over at her seat at the counter. "There was enough food for breakfast, then?"

Bea sat down their plates and took her own seat opposite her lover.

The two never used to share meals when Bea had worked for her. It wouldn't have felt professional, and Bea had always been far too self-conscious to stuff her face in front of so many prying eyes. She smiled a little at how natural something as simple as breakfast together could feel, despite the circumstances.

"There was more food than I thought, yes."

"Good." Evian dug into her plate. "So you can relax a little?"

"A little." Bea conceded. "But we should still proba-bly—"

"Wonderful." Evian cut her off. "Because I have plans for us today."

"Plans?"

It was just the two of them.

There was nothing to go do, no one left to see. There were only so many plans that could be conceived.

"Yes. We're going to go swimming."

"I still think we should talk about this."

"We are talking."

"We should make a plan. Even if the food holds out—which it won't forever—there are so many other things that could go wrong."

"You're worried about the water, right?" She nodded to the empty bottle next to the coffee pot.

"Very."

"Then come to the beach with me. Let me show you it's safe."

"I don't think that's a safe way to—"

"Bea?"

"Yes?"

"Will you please trust me?"

Bea was caught again between her desire to please Evi-an and her instinct to be honest with herself. One was stron-ger than the other, it seemed.

"I trust you."

"Good. I went through a lot of this stuff while you were sleeping, and I promise, we're going to be okay."

Hope sparked in her, real hope. "Oh. Well then you can tell me—"

"I don't like talking about this stuff. So, please, let me show you instead. Let me help you relax."

Bea opened her mouth to object, but the last embers of her resistance died when Evian met her eyes. She was too lovely to be denied.

"I want to relax," Bea said, too tired to argue any further.

"Good. Because I could really use a calming day after all the stress this week. I think it will be good for both of us."

Bea, who had been a big part of that stress, nodded along. "I'll try."

"Great. You can go get changed after breakfast."

"Get changed?"

"Into your swimsuit."

Bea looked down at her plate, that familiar insecurity gnawing away at the back of her brain. Perhaps she wasn't entirely cured after all. "I don't think I brought one."

"You came to an island getaway and you didn't pack a swimsuit?"

It sounded silly when phrased that way, but swimming hadn't ever come up once in the week prior to the end.

"I'm not a big fan of the water," she admitted.

"But it's so beautiful."

"I'll still go with you."

Evian tilted her head some, trying to get a read on her. "You'll just…watch me swim?" Her devious smile returned. "Is that something else you're into?"

"I can lie out on the sand. Do some tanning."

With her complexion, they both knew she'd burn rather than tan, but it would be worth it if it gave Evian the day she wanted.

"Are you sure?"

"Yeah. And I'll bring a…"

If you could bring five books with you to the desert island, which five would you bring?

Bea flinched and whipped her head around to look over shoulder.

The voice had echoed in her mind, but it had been so loud and clear that she expected to see the speaker standing behind her. There was only the kitchen.

"Bea?"

She looked back to Evian, and the concern furrowed on her brow. "Did… Did you hear something?"

"No." The rest of her partner's smile faded. "What did you hear?"

Bea didn't tell her that she'd heard the voice of her sister. What good would it do?

Her sister was dead.

Everyone is dead.

"Nothing," she said, and she stood up to clear the plates.

Evian caught her hand. "Come on. You need a day off as much as I do."

"I'm just going to clean up, and then I'll meet you out there."

Evian tugged her away, insistent. "No work today."

"But…"

"Bea, who cares if the dishes don't get done right away?"

Bea wanted to say that she cared, and she really didn't mind doing a couple dishes. But it was just one of those things that felt foolish in light of everything else.

"I guess I can get them later."

"Good."

Evian led her toward the door, then through the strange, dull living room.

The clock read 11:49 again—still.

Bea barely had time to register that it must be broken before Evian had the door open and their world was bathed in orange.

Things were so calm and curated inside the house that Bea had forgotten the sky was still on fire.

Evian's form was set ablaze as she stepped through the

door from the muted colors of their abode and into the deeply saturated inferno of the surrounding island.

Bea followed in her pajamas, through a small forest of palm trees that shaded the house. She wished they were a little better at their job, as she found the light to be unnerving. It was a bright reminder that the remnants of their small world were not, in fact, what she had known. It grew all the more pervasive as she was pulled along out from under the trees to the white, crunchy sand.

Bea held her tongue as Evian stripped down and went running for the water, alight with the reflection of the sky. She braced herself for a scream that never came. From where she stood it looked as though her lover had launched her whole body into a sea of molten lava.

But she reemerged, unharmed, and glittering in gold. She had never looked more divine.

Bea stretched out on the warm sand and watched for a long while. Sometimes her mind drifted off to the dark things. How she was certain she'd heard Elle's voice in the kitchen. How the two of them had never made amends, and now it was too late. She had failed miserably to protect someone she'd cared about, and it seemed an impossible injustice that she should be one of the two people in the world left standing.

But the thoughts were like the smoky clouds above her, wispy and intangible.

Watching the love of her life enjoying herself, Bea reminded herself to breathe. To enjoy. To relax. Evian dancing and splashing around in the water was what mattered now. It was something to distract. Something to live for.

With time, the orange atmosphere faded to a deep, blood red that made the clouds above look almost purple. Relief overtook her. It was not that she wanted the day to end. The day could have lasted forever, and Bea would have been content. It was rather that it was a relief to know that the sun was setting somewhere, even if she couldn't see it over the horizon. Something still existed that marked the passage of mortal time.

Perhaps the world was not all as broken as the clock.

6.

"Do you feel up to making dinner?"

"Yes." Bea felt more than a little pathetic for how she jumped—again—at the chance to do something useful, but it couldn't be helped. "What would you like?"

"How do you feel about pasta?"

Evian had changed first thing when they'd arrived back at the house, stripping off the bikini and slipping into a velvety nightgown. It might have been little more than lingerie, but it was plenty fancy enough that she deserved to eat a nice, Italian dinner while wearing it.

"Pasta sounds good…"

"I think there's some in the pantry." Evian offered when she heard the hesitation in Bea's voice.

"The…pantry?"

"You haven't seen it yet? I guess we never did take that tour."

They hadn't taken any kind of tour. Not of the house, anyway. Of each other's bodies though...

Bea had seen little enough of her new home, and even less of the surrounding island. The two had come in for their trip hot and heavy, and a tour hadn't seemed important.

"We were a little distracted," she admitted.

"Well let me show you."

Evian pulled her through to the kitchen, to the drink case. Bea watched, confused at first and then amazed as she gripped a discrete handle in the side and pulled the whole thing out—sparkling waters and all. The case swung out to reveal, of all things, a staircase.

Something shifted in Bea's brain.

Not for the first time, she felt the tide of dread threatening to snag her from the shore of sanity. The waves were getting stronger. What she was seeing didn't seem possible, even while she was staring straight at it.

As she looked down at a secret passage that had opened from the center of the kitchen, it all felt overwhelming. Surreal. Too good to be true. It was so dreamlike that she was apprehensive to make the descent, convinced she'd be committing herself to a fantasy world rather than a pantry.

It was, perhaps, not as grand as the whimsical world through the wardrobe she'd read about so often in her youth, but neither could the basement space be defined by the word "pantry."

The stairs descended into a large underground room, about half the size of the house above. Bea had seen convenience stores that were smaller and stocked with less. There were neat shelves of dried goods, grains, and labeled jars. Everything was airtight and well-preserved in the chilled room. Of course, it all appeared to be of the highest quality.

It was not enough food to last them the rest of their lives, but it was enough to make starvation feel like a distant problem.

She walked through in awe, and was too stunned to even be surprised when she saw a stone arch set into the far wall. Without needing to investigate, she saw how the space opened into a wine cellar. Doubtless, the bottles lurking there would each cost more than someone like her could comprehend.

Underneath the relief there was a sense of unease. The knowledge she didn't belong. Even knowing that the stockpile of goods may well be the thing sparing her, Bea's impoverished inner child could not help but look at the horde with some distaste for the manner in which the decadence had just been stashed away.

Unless…

"Are you okay?"

Bea turned around to find Evian's angelic form following her through the shelves. She was too pure a person to suspect of such a terrible scheme. "Yeah."

"You don't seem pleased?"

"This is just a lot. I didn't realize there was so much food here."

"Well that's a good thing." Evian paused. "Isn't it?"

"Of course it is." Bea did her best to shrug off any misgivings.

"Didn't I tell you we'd be okay?"

"You did."

"And you are okay, aren't you?"

"Yeah."

Evian reached a hand to Bea's cheek, then her forehead. "You don't look like you're doing so well."

A comment like that from Evian could have easily sent her spiraling on a better day, but if she were honest, Bea didn't feel like she was doing so well either. "I guess I'm getting pretty hungry too."

"Do you want me to make the pasta?"

"No," she said. "I've got it. What kind do you want?"

It rattled her that they had so many options.

Evian helped her carry the uncooked noodles and marinara upstairs, where she began to prepare dinner.

Cooking helped. It was only a small reprieve, but it was more than she could have expected given the circumstances. Productivity had always been her most effective coping technique, but there were only so many odd things her mind could shelve away. Keeping her hands busy kept her from falling apart, but it was not quite enough to drown out the memory of hearing a ghost in the kitchen earlier that day. It wasn't enough to forget the suspicions taking root in her about her lover.

It is simply too convenient. She owns this property. Why would she bring so much food for just two weeks?

"Do you need help with anything?"

"Yeah, if you could just grab the—" Bea cut herself off as she glanced over her shoulder at the counter, which already appeared to be cleaned off.

"Grab the what?" Evian asked.

Had she already washed the dishes from earlier? It wasn't possible. Bea hadn't gotten to the chore yet, and the two had been together all day, since she'd first been instructed to leave them.

"The wine. Would you go grab the wine?"

"Of course."

The second Evian was out of sight, Bea had the cupboard and the silverware drawer open so she could count plates and forks. There was a full, clean set of each, dried and put away. As if nothing had been touched at all.

"Don't worry about it," Evian said, before giving her a soft kiss on the cheek. Already she had returned from the basement, a bottle of wine in hand. "I'll set the table, you just worry about the food."

How many times had she dreamed about sharing such a night with Evian? This sort of closeness? This little slice of domestic bliss? More times than she could count. Yet now that it was happening, there were so many things out of place. Little things, but things, nonetheless. They shouldn't have mattered, but she couldn't quite help herself from noticing.

She was worried about the ghost.

And the dishes.

And what she'd seen in the cellar.

The terrible thoughts that now plagued her.

When she turned back, a pot of spaghetti in hand, she saw that Evian had dimmed the lights. It was not the flaming red of the world outside, but a warmer color than it had been, and accented with candles. The plates were set, and she was pouring them each a glass of wine.

Bea scooped the spaghetti noodles onto each of their plates before bringing over the last few things; a fresh salad lightly tossed with vinaigrette, butter, and a knife for the bread Evian had set out.

The candlelight danced on the edge of the metal.

"This might be heaven," Evian whispered after taking her first bite.

Bea sat a little straighter in her seat. "What?"

"Being here on the beach with nothing to do, and a beautiful woman cooking for me."

"Oh."

"I'm sorry I didn't help more," she said, seeming to sober up.

"It's not that."

Evian considered her, those eyes stripping Bea back to a shell. "But it is something?"

Bea couldn't deny that now. She felt as though her mind was fracturing, her thoughts spinning around like the noodles she kept twisting on her plate.

"Do you think... Is it possible that this all is a little too good?"

Evian's smile was sweet poison. "Nothing is too good for you."

"Evian..."

"No, no. I mean it. You deserve the best." She wanted that to be the end of the conversation, but it wasn't.

"Please, listen. I'm serious."

A storm flashed in Evian's eyes. "You're always serious," she snapped.

"I'm sorry..."

"You said you'd relax today."

"And I did. I have. I'm trying to, but—"

"But what?"

Timidity and guilt threatened to overtake her now that she was on the defensive, but a spell had been broken in the house. She felt the urgency to speak freely while she still felt capable of doing so. "Doesn't this all feel…"

"Feel what?"

"Too good?"

"I wish it did. I wish I could feel too good. But every time I start to forget what's happened, you start asking me all these terrible questions." Evian threw her fork down, splattering red sauce across the counter.

Bea recoiled. "I'm sorry."

"Are you? Because all I asked for was one day—"

"I know…"

"—and you said I could have it. You said that you trusted me!"

Thunder rumbled in the distance.

Bea could feel tears stinging her eyes. She felt like she might be swallowed whole by such anger. Still, Evian did not let up.

"We have been given this amazing chance. You and I. Just the two of us. The whole world was supposed to be wiped out, and you and I are still here. We're in this beautiful place, and we have food and water and one another, and I don't understand why you can't just be happy about it."

Bea didn't know why either.

She didn't know what was wrong with her, or why the perfect picture Evian had painted filled her with such dread. But it did. It felt wrong.

"Evian," she croaked.

47

"What?"

"Was it… Are we really here only by chance?"

"What are you talking about?"

"Please…don't be mad at me…but I have to ask…"

Evian watched her. Cold. Expectant.

"Did you know we'd survive?"

It wasn't surprise or pain that filled her gray-green eyes. The expression proved impossible to read. "Of course I didn't know."

"It's just…it seems like…"

"Seems like what, Bea? Hm?"

Bea balled her hands into fists, trying to work up the nerve to say it.

"If you want to accuse me of something," Evian said, "then do it."

"You seem so prepared and…and…"

"And what?"

"And I lost people, Evian."

It took both women by surprise when Bea burst into tears. She turned her face away in shame at the outburst, but was sniffling hard just to breathe. "If… If you knew what was happening…that we'd be safe here… I wish you would have told me. I wish… There were people I would have saved too."

Evian rose from her seat in slow motion—angelic, graceful—and Bea buried her face in her hands. But she couldn't stop now. It was all pouring out of her.

"I'll never see my sister again. I had so much to say to her, and now she's gone. And my mother. And...I won't be mad at you. I can never be mad at you if you saved me on purpose but...I want to know. And I wish you'd have told me. I wish I could understand any of this."

Evian had walked around the counter and was pulling Bea into her arms. She kept crying, even as her face was brought to Evian's chest. "Of course I didn't know that we'd survive."

"But the pantry is so full," she sobbed. "And the fridge."

"I had my staff stock it. Even I didn't know how much stuff was here until after you were sleeping, and I went to check."

It made sense that Evian wouldn't have done the preparation of the property herself. Of course she hadn't known.

"I just feel so guilty to be here," Bea tried to explain. She felt like she was pleading with Evian for her to understand emotions that were incomprehensible even to herself.

"I know. But it's not your fault."

"Everything is so overwhelming."

"I know."

"I just feel like I'm missing something. I shouldn't have accused you, but do you really not feel it?"

"We just went through a big change. I think you're probably in shock. I know I had a tough time at first, but it gets better."

Evian had only had a two-day head start. Bea couldn't imagine feeling that much better in two days.

"Do you promise?"

"I do. But it helps if you don't dwell on all the bad things."

Bea didn't feel like it was even possible to dwell on something that she hadn't processed yet. But Evian's words were almost as soothing as her hands, which were rubbing over Bea's back to relieve the tension. Her fingers—instruments of pleasure—caressed her through her shirt.

"I know it's scary to be here. But we're here now. I feel so lucky to be sharing this time with you. I don't want to waste it fighting. I think we should just make the best of it."

"I do too." Even though Bea meant it, there was just one more thing she had to mention. "Evian?"

"Yes?"

"Can I ask you one more question?"

"Anything."

"When did you clear the dishes?"

Thunder rumbled again, and this time it sounded as though it were directly overhead.

Evian's embrace on her went limp, and her voice was cold when she spoke again. "What dishes?"

"From breakfast. You told me not to get them. But when we came in…"

"You cleaned up before we went out. Remember?"

"No...I didn't."

"I thought you trusted me, Bea."

"I'm just trying to understand. If I didn't get them, and you didn't get them—"

"I thought you wanted this to work." Evian sounded so despondent.

Bea pulled away, hoping to search her eyes for any clue as to what was happening. No sooner had she straightened up, however, than she felt a knife slide into her gut.

The rain was coming down in sheets, and she could hear it battering the roof of the house. There were tears in Evian's eyes, blood on her hands, sorrow on her trembling lips. "Why can't you just let this be beautiful?"

This page left intentionally blank

Part 2

7.

What was left of the world was hazy. Bea woke up dazed, with a cotton-dry mouth and no sense of where she was or what was happening. She felt a vague notion she'd been through all of that before.

She didn't question the luxurious surroundings or try to make sense of the nightmare she'd been having. The lines between her dreams and waking hours were too blurred together to waste energy on trying to separate.

Coffee, she hoped, would clear things up and it seemed her body was already carrying her in that direction. The heavy scent of roasted beans wafted through the hallway, and she was content to follow her nose.

"There you are, sleepyhead." Evian chirped when she entered the kitchen. "You feeling any better?"

Bea couldn't remember feeling bad. There was only the faintest recollection of heaviness, combined with the still-present pins-and-needles sensation over her entire body that grew more powerful when she gave it attention.

"Bea?"

"Yeah?" Bea slumped into a seat at the kitchen counter usually taken by Evian herself—the seat facing the kitchen.

Evian's eyes were soft, but piercing. "Are you feeling better today?"

"Oh." She thought she answered, but maybe she had just been standing there. "I guess."

"You don't know?"

"I feel alright. I don't remember really feeling bad."

Evian poured a fresh cup of coffee and handed it to her with a sweet, sympathetic smile. "Maybe this will help you clear your head."

"Maybe."

The warm cup was pleasant between her hands, and she found it was much easier to focus. Her senses were alright, it was just her mind that was running around untamed.

She took a sip and savored the smooth taste.

"Better?"

It was the third time Evian had inquired after her well-being since she had stepped into the kitchen.

"Yeah. But I don't remember what happened." She confessed.

There was that smile from the blonde again, the strange one. It looked less empathetic the second time around, and more pitying.

"I'm not surprised. You had an awful lot to drink the other night."

"Oh." She took another sip. "Did I?"

Evian tilted her head to the side. "You really can't remember?"

Bea tried. She really tried to think about it.

She remembered falling asleep tangled around Evian, and waking up with the worst hangover of her life. She remembered a white-sand beach, and something about a wine cellar. It came as an almost underwhelming afterthought that the entire world had ended somewhere during that time.

That was becoming a fact she just took for granted.

"I remember some things. I think we were going to take a tour of the house?"

Evian laughed a little. "That much is gone, huh?"

Bea didn't admit she didn't even have that much. "You've got to quit letting me drink." She tried to say it with a chuckle of her own, but the truth was she wasn't kidding.

The other day, Evian had said, implying Bea had been in a stupor for longer than she'd realized. And she had a vague impression this wasn't the first occasion she had lost time.

"But you blush so easily when you drink." Evian teased her. "It's cute."

She stepped close and put a hand on Bea's back in an intimate gesture, her graceful fingers lingering between Bea's shoulder blades. Such a touch would have once sent sparks through her body but, instead, she tensed up. Her palms began to sweat around her coffee mug.

"I don't think it's the alcohol that makes me blush." Her tone didn't hit the intended target of flirting, her voice thin and empty.

"Oh?"

"You've never touched me like this before."

Bea was certain she'd be blushing at such familiarity, were it not for the crawling sensation on her skin that warned of danger.

Evian seemed to feel her tension, and pulled away. But she gave her another curious look. "Haven't I?"

Bea didn't bother searching her memories for confirmation one way or the other. They weren't under her control that day, and she was tired already of proving as much. "Maybe."

Chuckling, Evian pulled herself away, as if she found the whole situation endearing. "Finish up your coffee. Can I get you anything to eat?"

"I can get something."

"Nonsense, you're sitting. Eggs? Toast?"

"Sure," she agreed.

It felt like a lifetime ago she'd been the one making

Evian breakfast in that kitchen. For all she knew, it had been a lifetime.

She found herself leaning back in her chair, trying to get a look at the clock in the adjacent room. The half wall dividing the kitchen from the living room blocked her view.

"Do you want more coffee?"

"No, I'm alright."

Evian was already refilling her cup though, so she drank it down and then started at the food that was placed before her. She felt like it was finished rather fast, but it was hard to tell. Time as a concept was meaning less and less.

"What do you want to do today?"

Bea shrugged, between bites of egg. "What can we do?"

She hadn't packed much in the way of entertainment as far as she knew. There hadn't been much time to prepare her choices, and she had come to the island expecting it to be a short stay.

"We can do anything you want."

Bea couldn't explain why, but Evian's smile looked like an apology.

She was reminded of a game she and her sister used to play. The Desert Island Game.

If you were trapped on a desert island and you could only bring five books...

Five movies...

Five albums…

She could not help but to burst into laughter when she realized. How many countless hours of her youth had she spent agonizing over such lists, weighing her options, updating her rankings up to five slots? How disappointed would that child have been to learn she would grow into an adult who would bring nothing with her to the island? There Bea sat, laughing like a madwoman, woefully devoid of entertainment options.

"What's so funny?" Evian asked.

That only made it funnier, because for a minute, Bea had forgotten she wasn't alone. Her side burned as she kept laughing so hard she struggled to breathe, and it was a long time before she could answer. "Sorry," she said. "Sorry. I just didn't bring any books with me."

That sounded funny too.

Evian cocked her head to one side and tried to search for any traces of the joke. "Do you want to read?"

"No, I only…" Bea had an absurd, terrible thought then.

She believed, was certain in fact, that if she said yes to reading, Evian would have found her a book to read. She was equally positive, though it was contradictory, that there were— at that moment—no books on the island. They wouldn't be there until she admitted she wanted them.

It made no sense. Yet she believed it to her core.

"Are you okay?" Evian asked her for a fourth time.

"Probably still a little drunk, is all."

Evian's brow furrowed.

She knew Bea had not been drunk in the first place, just as Bea was realizing she hadn't been drunk. For two different reasons, neither woman could admit to the lie they were now both aware of. The tension between them lingered a moment.

"We could go out to the beach?" Evian suggested.

Déjà vu washed over Bea, but she nodded. "Yeah. I'd like that."

She wasn't much of a swimmer, but she liked the fresh air and the sand. She liked watching Evian. She didn't know what she'd do for a swimsuit, though.

"I can lend you one if you want?"

Bea set her fork down. "What?"

"A swimsuit? You said you didn't have one."

"Oh." Bea wondered when exactly she had said that. The other day, probably, before the night when she'd allegedly had too much to drink. That would have been the last day she'd been saying much of anything, before all the time had gone missing.

She had the nagging sense the two of them had been on the beach that day, too. She wished she could remember how long ago that had actually been, or how long they'd really been on the island.

"So?" Evian's voice snapped her out of such thoughts.

"So what?"

"Would you like to borrow a swimsuit?"

"Oh. No," she answered. "Thanks, but I don't think any of yours would fit me."

"You never know until we try." Evian winked, but she seemed content to drop the subject after that.

Bea stood up to clear her plate.

"Leave it," Evian told her.

She was certain they'd been through all of that already. This time she didn't fight it. She didn't argue or object or ask what had happened to the last plates she'd left out. She just set the plate back down on the counter and followed Evian away from the kitchen.

She glanced up at the wall on her way through, expecting the clock to read 11:49.

But there was no clock.

There was just a slight, gray discoloration in the white paint where a clock had been.

The world outside was still orange, but brighter today. The wispy clouds had all but vanished from the sky above.

Bea sat on the warm, white sand, and stared up at it for a while. As it always did, her attention soon turned back to Evian.

The love of her life.

She was a sight to see, of course. Long and tan, she

moved through the mirror surface of the still water with all the grace of a mermaid. She was as close to perfect as anyone could be, though Bea knew it was not half so effortless as she made it look. Her hair and makeup were done again, and each minute that she maneuvered brought a new dynamic to her flattering poses.

Bea wondered if Evian would still be trying so hard to maintain her polished image if she were on the island alone. Maybe it was so ingrained in her that she didn't remember any other way to be. Or maybe, possibly, Evian had brought her along for the sole purpose of having an audience—so she felt there was a reason to keep up her appearances. It would make sense that Bea would have been chosen for the task of spectator above anyone else. It was a role she had always been devoted to.

There were worse things in life to be, if that's all she was. Rather than to question it, Bea could feel herself tempted to give into the position. To just settle down in the sand and let the simplicity of such an existence wash over her.

Her side still hurt from where she had laughed too hard earlier. Rubbing at the spot, her fingers lingered over the rough bump of scar tissue.

8.

On the mainland, before the end, Bea had considered herself a morning person. When she woke up on the island to find Evian still sleeping, however, she was surprised. There was a feeling of disconnect between the version of herself that was there, surviving, and the version of herself she'd known up until that point. A pang went through her heart, to find she was a stranger to herself.

Then again, everything had come with a healthy dose of strange since the end had not successfully ended things.

Bea was careful as she slid out of the bed and padded to the bathroom. Luckily, the master bedroom was covered in a plush carpet that dampened the sound of her footsteps. This was different from the floors in the other rooms. At least, the other rooms she had seen. Despite the fact she was now living on the island, she had yet to explore even half the property. That was something she hoped to fix, and with any luck, she could do so without waking Evian. There was just one thing she wanted to attend to first.

When the door had been pulled quietly behind her, Bea switched on the bathroom light. She was surprised by her image in the large mirror, at how normal her reflection looked. It wasn't that she felt bad, exactly, but she had been through so much since last she'd gotten a look at herself. It felt remarkable that such experiences had not taken a physical toll.

She lifted up her T-shirt over her belly and studied the skin. It was pale in comparison to the recently tanned, nearly burnt skin of her arms. It was also smooth, unblemished. She squinted at herself, tugging at the skin where she expected a scar.

She watched her reflection do the same, but there was no line, no mark of what she had felt yesterday. She could feel the rough skin beneath her fingers, but it looked fine in the mirror. She twisted some, crossing one arm over her chest to try and flatten out her breasts so she could get a better, direct look at the area. Such a task proved beyond her.

The scar she was looking for was on the underside of where her stomach curved, and there was no good way to flatten it out with one hand while also pressing on her chest, and not obstructing the view somewhere in the process.

Not for the first time, Bea found herself cursing her

body, her weight, and this time it had nothing to do with how she looked. Who cared if she was big? She just wanted to see the scar she could so clearly feel. She wanted to know if her reflection matched herself. She wanted to understand.

She brushed her fingers over the diagonal line of jagged skin, running between her belly button and her hip bone.

After another minute of contorting, she gave up, knowing it was useless and not wanting to be discovered there. There was exploration to be done before Evian woke.

She lowered her shirt back over the top of her shorts and turned the light off before creeping back through the bedroom. With each step she grew more conscious of her weight, her breathing, and every stray sound her body made. She only let the tension ease—and only a little—when she was in the hallway with the door closed behind her.

I am not a prisoner here.

She tried not only to remind herself of the fact, but to believe it as she walked away from the bedroom. Her heart and her mind were both racing.

There was a familiar urge rising within her to keep busy—an old coping mechanism that had never failed her in the past. She took the long way around to the kitchen, the path that looped her through the living room and back around through the far side of the dining area. She looked to the discoloration on the wall where she was sure a clock had once read 11:49. All the while she kept an eye out for something in the pristine house that could use her attention.

She allowed herself to detour to the front door, holding her breath as she cracked it open. The smell was right; clean and fresh, a saltwater breeze that had been filtered through the surrounding palm trees. The color was all wrong, though, the light pouring like spilt wine into the clean interior of the house.

Bea pulled her head back inside and closed the door once again.

Her hands were fidgeting as she made her way to the kitchen, looking for something to tidy or straighten. There was no mess. No crumbs, no trace that the room had ever been used. The dishes were no longer sitting out from yesterday.

Evian was still asleep. She would not have had the time to clean them, even if she'd had the inclination to do so.

Bea shook her head and opened the fridge. She wasn't sure what to think about the situation. Something was amiss—but she had no idea what the oddities added up to. She meant to consider it over a glass of orange juice, and was already reaching for the carton when her hand stopped.

She went instead for the top carton of eggs.

After checking its contents, she opened the other three cartons.

Not a single egg was missing from any of the four, though she remembered eating scrambled eggs for breakfast the day before. She had another hazy recollection of cooking omelets herself.

She closed the cartons back up and replaced them, trying to work through it. It would have been impossible to order in new eggs, which left the distinct reality that Bea was losing her mind. It was almost a relief, to let the idea of control slip away.

"I may just lose touch with reality," she heard a voice, suspiciously like her own, mumble from the couch.

"Would that be so bad?"

Evian.

Bea rushed around the half wall that blocked her view to the couch, following the voices with determination, even as she remembered already having the conversation which now graced her ears. She entered the space to find the living room empty.

Of course. She began moving again, turning to the coat rack in the otherwise sparse room. Hanging from it were the only two things she could see that she remembered seeing brought into the house with her own two eyes.

Evian's unseasonably warm but undeniably stylish black leather cropped jacket hung up beside her own, more practical rain slicker. Bea stuck her hand into first one, then the other pocket, certain that was where she had last stashed her phone. She tried the other side, then rechecked before resorting to rifling through Evian's coat as well. Empty.

She looked around on the floor to where her cell may have fallen, then under the furniture and in between couch cushions. It didn't make sense to her that the phone would be missing; she hadn't touched it. There was only one other person who might have moved it, but for what purpose?

Bea had a tough time imagining Evian would hide her phone. But then again, there was a reason why she was performing her investigation before dawn, when she could be alone. The reason took the form of a scar, a nightmare she couldn't quite remember, a distrust in her partner she was too afraid to name.

The accusation lingered at the tip of her tongue, but even in her head the words could not take shape until she had a clearer picture of what was going on. She needed more pieces of the puzzle, and felt like her phone may have answers that she needed.

The house, with its missing clock and replenishing eggs, was too artificial. It was like a set Evian had staged for her social media feed; curated to perfection. Something—someone—was trying to make her forget the outside world, and what had come before. She wasn't being permitted to think about the bad thing that had happened.

What did happen? How did it—

Bea was certain if she could reach out, and see the ruin for herself, get some news, understand the state of the world better, that the spell cast over her would be broken.

Desperate now, she searched for a landline. A clock. Her phone. Her tablet. Any of Evian's electronics, of which countless had surely been brought.

Nothing.

There was no trace of time, nothing to connect her to whatever still lingered off the island.

Caution was gradually lost as she went about her search, looking through more and more of the house. There was a pristine guest room where she remembered vomiting up her guts for two days. Across from that was another bedroom, and then another, and one more bathroom.

At the end of the long hall was a final door, different from the others. It was made of thick, frosted glass, and Bea couldn't tell what was on the other side. She tried her hand at opening it, only to find it locked.

"What are you doing?"

Bea couldn't help but jump as she turned around to face Evian. "I...was just looking for our things."

Surely that was allowed, right? Expected, even? Only why then, did she feel so afraid to tell her lover the truth?

"They're in our room," the blonde said. Calm.

"Are they? I must have missed them."

She hadn't bothered looking, in truth. The bedroom was so sparse and familiar that it had not seemed worth her time to search — never mind that it had posed the danger of waking Evian.

"Of course."

"Right," she said as she pushed past the other woman, holding in a nervous breath. Their shoulders scraped against one another, as Evian did not move aside to let her pass. "I'll just go get them, then."

"What do you need?"

"What?"

"Out of our things. What are you looking for?"

Bea barely even considered lying. She was a terrible liar, which kept her honest by all but omission. "My phone."

One perfect eyebrow arched in confusion, and the air felt like static between them. "Who are you planning on calling?"

"No one. I just wanted to see my phone."

"The phones would be dead by now anyway."

Odd choice of words.

Would be. Like they were gone.

"There are chargers." She pointed out.

"But no service."

"Did you check?"

The silence grew deafening.

Bea felt emboldened by it, and repeated her question. "Did you check?"

"We're the only ones left, Bea."

"You can't know that," she said, the horror of that information sinking in.

"But I do."

"Even if there was no service—"

"It's all gone."

"But how do you—"

"Of course I checked," Evian snapped. One perfect tear rolled down her cheek. "While you were in bed, sick. I did everything that could be done. I tried to get help for us. For you. But there's no one left. It's just us, and I don't know if I can go through all that false hope in trying again. It was horrible. I can't do that."

Bea wondered if the tear was real.

How many times had she watched such emotions be conjured for the camera out of thin air? But there were no cameras anymore, no technology at all, it seemed. The fact hammered in Evian's words.

It's just us.

Real or not, Bea found herself succumbing to the tear. To Evian. "I'm sorry," she said.

"Can we please just relax for now? Just for today?"

Bea recalled that relaxing for just one day was all Evian had wanted yesterday too, but it didn't matter. "Okay."

Evian brushed the tear away. "Do you want some breakfast?"

"Okay."

Numb, Bea followed her lover to a kitchen that she knew was fully stocked with eggs.

9.

Bea couldn't help but to pick at her food. It smelled delicious, but that was part of the problem. Remembering how it had all just appeared in the fridge, she couldn't help but wonder if it was too good to be true. She ended up pushing the same bite around her plate, absentminded, as she watched Evian. Her partner was eating yogurt, topped with berries.

They were as fresh as they had been at the beginning of the week, looking as though they had just been picked that morning. Bea couldn't keep herself from staring at them.

"Are you okay?"

Bea nodded.

"You're not eating."

Bea shrugged. "I guess I'm just not that hungry."

"Are you still feeling sick? Hungover?"

Bea wanted to scream that she hadn't been sick in days, that she could not remember being hungover the last time she'd been ill. That she resented the implication she had a problem when in fact, she'd be happier never having another drop of alcohol for as long as she lived.

She suppressed the outburst with another shrug.

"Bea, tell me what's wrong."

Not a question.

"You won't want to hear it."

Bea knew how sulky she sounded, but she had already exceeded her limit of things that could bother her.

"Of course I want to hear it." Evian reached across the counter to take her hands, but Bea pulled away. She sat up straighter and let her arms fall to her sides, the breakfast now forgotten.

"No." She insisted. "You won't. Whenever I try to talk to you about the serious stuff, you put it off, and pull away, and make me feel terrible."

And you stab me, she almost added, but she caught herself, unsure of where the thought had come from.

"I just don't like to think about the bad stuff," Evian said, wounded. As though it were something that could be easily put behind them. "We've been through enough bad things for a lifetime. Is it so wrong I want to focus on the good stuff, now that it's just the two of us and we're here?"

"I'm not through the bad stuff yet, Evian."

"But we are."

"I'm not through it yet," she repeated, firmer.

Evian sat down her spoon, scowling. She had never been a woman who was reasonable when things didn't go her way.

Trying again, with a gentleness she wasn't sure she still felt, Bea continued. "I want to be happy here. I want to enjoy this time with you. But I need to process everything that's happened. Nothing feels real anymore."

Evian did that thing she did so well, where she stepped into the role of victim. "I don't feel real?"

For once, Bea didn't back down or let herself lose control of the conversation. "No, you don't. Nothing does. The world ended, Evian. I didn't expect to just keep going after it was supposed to be all gone. I don't know what's supposed to happen now, what we're supposed to do."

"Whatever we want."

As if it were easy.

"But I don't know what I want."

"I think you know exactly what you want, and I think that scares you."

Of all the things she expected to be accused of, that just wasn't one of them. "What the hell is that supposed to mean?"

"You let me do things—hell, you asked me to do things to you that last night we shared. Do you remember that?"

How could she ever forget? Her cheeks were still burning at the mere mention of such acts.

"I do, but—"

"I think you'd be happier if we had never stopped. You told me before it was just a morbid curiosity, that you wanted to try it just once before we died. But you liked it, didn't you?"

"Evian…"

"Didn't you?"

Bea bit her lip, trying hard not to let herself get sidetracked by such thoughts. Whether she liked it or not, that wasn't the point. "I did, only…"

Before Bea had a chance to object, Evian was up and around the counter, grabbing Bea's hands before she could think of a coherent end to her argument. "Wouldn't you like to just let me take care of things?"

Bea closed her eyes. She hoped it would give her clarity, but her mind flooded with memories instead. She remembered how gorgeous Evian had looked naked, gazing down from atop her. She remembered how good it had felt—how oddly freeing—to be at her mercy. "I would…but—"

"Then let me," Evian growled. Once again, her voice was a low command from the back of her throat. "Stop worrying about everything. Let me take care of you."

Take care of you.

It sounded so familiar.

The déjà vu tangled in her desire, making her feel lost, and her desire feel inevitable. It was threatening her sanity just how tempting it was to give in.

She could see Evian stripping her bare, pulling her along to the master bedroom where she would be tied down and teased. She'd known that pleasure only briefly, but it had been the best night of her life, even as she had lost everything else. It hadn't mattered then that the world was burning. So what should it matter now? What could be more important than the lust in her lover's eyes, the feeling of their bodies pressed into one flesh?

Opening her eyes to keep herself from drowning in the fantasy, Bea said, "I want to. But I just... Please...I need to work through a couple things first."

Evian went cold in an instant, her expression emotionless as she dropped Bea's hands. "Fine."

Bea wondered if it was the first real rejection the woman had ever had. Most certainly it was the largest. Nothing short of an apocalypse would enable any man or woman to refuse such a tempting offer from her.

Even though it had been a victory on her part, Bea found she already regretted her strength. "Just give me a couple days," she said. "Let me work through the issues I'm having. I need to come to terms with everything."

"And then what?" Evian snapped.

Bea had only seen glimpses of this anger in her, and

she couldn't help but shrink back under such ire. She hoped the storm would pass soon.

"Then I'll be able to move on. I'll be able to enjoy whatever time we have left."

"We have all the time in the world."

"Then let me have a day or two to get through this." She could see the anger in Evian's eyes giving way at the thought. She felt bold enough to press the advantage. "And then we can figure out what we want."

"I know what I want."

"Then wait for me to catch up to you. Please?"

Bea stared at her until—after an eternity—Evian met her eyes. They only needed to lock their gaze for a brief moment before the blonde surrendered with a sigh. "Fine. Sure. A couple days. But I don't understand what it is you hope to accomplish by waiting."

"I don't either. That's one of the things I want to understand."

Evian shook her head and turned her back on Bea, walking away through the kitchen. She left her dishes unattended on the counter. Without needing to be told, Bea did the same.

10.

Bea didn't think it was a coincidence that Evian walked back into the house after agreeing to give her space—closing herself off in the very room she'd told Bea she was keeping their things. It was alright, though.

Bea had just as many questions about the outside of the island.

She would not consider herself to be an explorer. Even at home, with terrain she knew well, she was hardly an outside person. Nature could be terrifying, but she hoped that today it would help her put some things into perspective.

She walked through the trees to the large stretch of sand where she'd been tanning just yesterday. The day had brightened up to a fresh, almost citrusy orange that felt deceptively natural. Would the clouds above them ever start to fade? Would they take with them her memories of when the sky had been blue? Was it possible she could live long enough to forget?

That was something she struggled with; living long-term on the island. Such a fate—and with Evian no less—could have easily passed as her concept of Heaven just a week or so before. Now, with the fighting, and the eeriness of her situation, she was less sure.

It was not that the future of staying there was so terrible, or that it scared her exactly. It was just difficult for her to imagine. Any sort of future was.

Evian had been able to instill in her mind such a vivid image of what an entire life of pain and pleasure might look like, but Bea found she had no luck conjuring up an alternative scenario of her own; better or worse.

Would she even be choosing a life with Evian if there was no other choice? Or had she already made her decision by coming on the trip in the first place?

The island sands couldn't answer the big questions, obviously, or clear up the matter of her future. She hoped, however, they could shine some light on her past.

About how they had gotten there.

About how, if they wanted to, they might be able to leave.

Bea took off counterclockwise along the shore. It bothered her more than a little that she had no strong idea of what she was looking for. A boat? A dock? Surely there must have been something similar when they had arrived, but it was strange she couldn't remember.

The goal was just to find something—anything—that could jog her memories of arrival. A landmark. A feeling. Anything. The more she tried to remember first seeing the island, her early impressions of it, the more such thoughts slipped through her fingers. It was very much like a dream in that regard.

Her mind kept wandering back to the jackets on the coatrack near the door, where she had first discovered her phone was missing. Had it been cold when they'd arrived? Raining? That didn't seem right, but the earliest memory she had was stripping off the coat, phone still in the pocket, to hang up at the door.

That had only been a week or so ago. How could she not remember what had happened just before that? The weather? The boat? Her clothes underneath the jacket?

Was I wearing jeans? A dress?

There was a pang in her chest as she tried to summon up the thought process that had surely gone into her outfit—something the old Bea would no doubt have obsessed over. How many hours over the last year must she have spent spinning around in front of her mirror, fixated on her stomach? She had always obsessed over what would hide her best, while also looking professional, only for it not to matter. No one ever looked her way when she stood in a space with Evian.

The recurring pattern of insecurity and helplessness had left a shadow in her brain, but the specifics had washed away. She was severed from that version of herself.

The Bea who walked along the beach now had snuck out of bed, eaten, and left the house all in front of Evian, all without thinking about her clothes or how she looked in them.

Come to think of it, she wasn't sure the last time she had changed out of her plaid lounge shorts and her favorite, soft gray tee.

The outfit smelled clean enough, but it was all she had worn during her stay on the island, if memory served.

Was it possible she'd been wearing it when she'd gotten sick?

When she'd been stabbed?

That horrid flash raced through her mind again; Evian holding a knife that twisted in her intestines which shone as red and wet as the pasta on the counter between them.

Bea stopped to collect her breath at such a thought, feeling exposed and overheated. She looked up to see how far she had made it, only to realize that the view looked the same as when she had set out.

A glance over her shoulders brought the information that she'd left no tracks in the dry sand behind her, as if they had been washed away by the still waters. When she looked ahead of her once more, all she saw was the same, gentle curvature of the island.

She kept walking, keeping her eyes peeled for any sign of the house on her left, or any other structure for that matter.

The sky indicated it was still daytime, but she felt as though she'd been walking for a couple hours at least when she finally came across something; Evian was swimming in the distance up ahead.

The terrible realization that she could walk around the entirety of her new existence in a single morning left her struggling to breathe the salty air.

Why did the island have to be so small? So strange? How could the two of them ever make it in such a place?

Not ready to go inside, and definitely not feeling up to another conversation with Evian, Bea turned around to go back the way she had come.

She took her time, savoring the solitude, making it last. No longer was she on an active hunt for clues that she knew she wouldn't find, and she tried to revel in the silence. If she had gotten hungry or thirsty she may have sped up her crawl of a pace, but she seemed to be past such things at the moment.

What was not beyond her was worry. The sense of dread only increased as the sky finally started to darken. It was a fiery red by the time she saw Evian once more, the clear water aflame by means of its reflection. It looked as hot as ever, like it should be boiling.

As she drew closer she could see a deeper, darker red, clouding under the surface where Evian tread water.

She rushed forward in her panic. "Evian?"

Evian turned to her, waiting with a wide smile. "Bea!" she called. "How was your walk?"

Bea stopped, staring in horror.

Evian's stomach was blistered and bubbling, her insides leaking into the surrounding water. The skin of her legs was even worse, practically non-existent in some places, slick and shining with blood in others.

"Are you okay?" she asked, hoarse.

Evian cocked her head to the side. "Why wouldn't I be okay?"

Bea didn't know how to tell her. She just kept staring down at the cords of muscle exposed in the burning woman's upper thigh.

"Oh, because of our fight this morning? I think I get it now. You just needed a little time."

She took a step forward and a large patch of angry skin sloughed off from above her knee. Bea found herself taking a step back. "I...am glad you understand."

"Are you feeling any better now?"

As more of her skin came floating above the surface of the water, Bea could smell the infection, the yellow pus leaking from every burst bubble of the burn.

"Yeah, maybe. I cleared my head some, I guess."

She was still retreating, mortified. Would it be worse if Evian looked down and started screaming in agony? Or if she couldn't see at all what was happening?

"Do you want to come join me?" Evian smirked.

"No." Bea shook her head. "I think I'm going to just head on inside. Maybe do some reading."

"Are you sure?"

More and more of her was coming out of the water, twisted, and leaking. She was a bloody skeleton in a black two-piece.

"Yeah, I'm sure. I'll see you back at the house."

She turned and started making her way to the tree line.

"The water's fine!" Evian called. Her voice sounded miles away, but Bea didn't bother looking back at her to check.

11.

Another night.
Another morning.

More weirdness.

Bea woke up, not ill, but not well, either. There was a book propped open over her chest, and she was lying in the strange guest room. This time, she was pretty sure she herself had chosen to sleep there.

The memories of what had happened were vague, but the emotions behind them were real. This was how all her context seemed these days. There had been anger at Evian for trapping them in such a place, fear for the way she ignored her body burning. She'd come into the house panicked, with the intention of tossing the master bedroom until she found her phone.

Then the book.

Though Bea had fallen asleep reading it just the night before, she couldn't recall the title or what had been going on in the tome. She just remembered the feelings associated with finding it. It had soothed her anger and left dread in its wake.

Why?

Because she didn't know where it had come from.

Because she believed Evian had summoned it somehow into existence to distract her from finding her things, or taking stock of what was missing.

She had fallen asleep reading the book in a nonsensical attempt to prove to herself that the book was real, and now all she could recall was that she had been reading it.

The whole experience worked only in the abstract sense, with dream logic. They were not the real actions of a flesh and blood, sensible person. Bea wasn't sure if such a description applied to her anymore.

She picked up the book and considered the cover. She flipped through the pages and read some of the words.

They were real.

Yet they were white noise in her brain.

She stopped trying to read the book or remember the details of how it had come into her possession. She sat up and reached for the bag she'd packed, and dragged into the spare bedroom with her the night before. She already knew, without knowing, that her electronics would be missing. There was never anything in the house that would give her the precise time—not since the clock had gone missing.

But there were other things. Tangible things. Real items from off the island that she felt she could trust.

As she took inventory, she became increasingly aware that such actions and thought patterns were not the kind that could be expected from a rational person.

There were not many possessions in the bag. It contained only a change of proper clothes, some additional sleepwear, her toiletries, and a photograph in a small, silver, novelty frame.

She tried to remember her thought process in bringing these things, certain it held clues that could be important. But had it been? Or had she given it any thought at all, believing that she wouldn't live long enough for any of it to matter? That seemed to be the only feeling she could associate with her frame of mind right before the end; that nothing much had mattered.

She looked at the picture a little closer. The woman in it looked like her, but younger, and slimmer, and sporting gorgeous highlights in her dark hair. She had a big smile on her face, like nothing terrible had ever, or would ever happen to her.

But hadn't it?

Bea knew that the woman pictured was her sister, and that something terrible had, in fact, happened. Even before the terrible thing that had happened to the whole world—something she felt vaguely responsible for.

But she couldn't remember what it was.

She couldn't even remember her sister's name.

A cold sense of remorse washed over her that she could have already forgotten the name of the most important person in her life other than Evian. Before it could be replaced with panic, there was a knock at the door.

She pushed the frame deep into her bag and covered it with the spare clothes before getting out of bed to answer it.

Evian was on the other side, picture-perfect in her creamy silk sleep set. "I hope I didn't wake you?"

"No," Bea said. "I was up."

"I was wondering if you wanted to have breakfast with me?"

Bea almost asked what time it was, but she caught herself. Either Evian was trapped there with her and wouldn't know the time, or she was the reason that the clocks and electronics were all missing. Either way, the question would be pointless.

"Bea?"

She realized she was just standing there, and it was taking her a long time to work through the issue. She had the same mental fog she'd associated with her island hangovers, but she'd be damned if she was going to admit to such a thing, or let Evian accuse her of drinking too much again. This time she knew for a fact she hadn't.

"Breakfast would be great," she said.

"Eggs?"

Her stomach roiled. She wasn't sure she wanted anything from that kitchen, but especially not the eternally spawning eggs. She tried to think of a food they didn't have in the kitchen, and then she realized that was perfect. She was being given the opportunity to test Evian, and this weird house.

"Coffee," she said, to buy time as she thought it over. She ran through a mental list of the kitchen's inventory and eventually came up with a food that wasn't on it. "Are there bagels? With cream cheese?"

She already knew there weren't, but Evian nodded. "I think so. I can check. Do you want me to bring that to you in bed?"

"No!" she answered, a little too quickly. "No, I'll meet you out there in just a few."

"You sure?"

"Yeah. I just want to get dressed. We can eat together."

Evian beamed at her. "Perfect. I'll go get it ready, then."

Bea waited until she was gone to get dressed in the one change of clothes she had. She wriggled into the comfiest pair of pants she'd ever owned, but was distracted by how rough the fabric felt against her legs in comparison to the shorts she'd been lounging in. The sensation was hard to describe, but the fabric felt heavier than it should have, too stark in contrast.

Dressing in her own things that she had brought from her home onto the island gave her the strength she needed to proceed. She had the feeling the day was going to be another trial.

Evian had a cup of coffee and a bagel with cream cheese already waiting for her on the counter. Because of course she did.

Bea forced herself to consume the breakfast, turning the bagel over in her mouth as she chewed. It tasted real enough—good, even. But it wasn't possible. As she watched Evian eat her açaí bowl, she recalled that those were all at least ingredients that had been stocked in the magical fridge.

"How are you doing?" Evian asked her.

She forced a smile. "Better."

"I was worried about you yesterday. You didn't look so good."

Bea didn't think she was one to talk. Evian's long legs looked fine and tanned today, but Bea didn't think she'd been dreaming when she'd watched them burn just the day before, no matter how reminiscent the memory was of a nightmare.

"There's just a lot to take in," she said.

"But you're working through that, aren't you?"

Was she?

She nodded. "I think so. I had some time to think,

and now I just want to sit with it awhile. I think I'll take it easy today. Maybe try to relax."

Evian smirked. "Maybe read?"

Bea could not help but wonder if that was a taunt. Her unease about the book flooded back to her. She had mentioned reading in passing outside during the feverish scene on the beach, and when she had gotten in there had been a mysterious book waiting for her. Almost as if Evian had known she'd bring up the pastime and laid it out for her.

Or like she had summoned it.

"Maybe," she answered. She thought about how to broach the subject, without making it another one of their serious talks, which would escalate into a fight. "I did quite a bit of reading last night, though. I'm almost through my book."

"You read fast."

Bea shrugged.

Over Evian's shoulder, she saw the girl from the photo standing in the kitchen.

"If you were trapped on a desert island and could only bring five books…"

"It's easy to read when I have a lot of time," she said.

Evian sat down her bowl and spoon. "Listen," she said. "About yesterday."

Despite everything, Bea was expecting her to confess that she had conjured the book out of thin air, or burned her legs, or killed Bea last week. All of the strange flashes of absurdity ran through her mind, and part of her expected Evian to admit to them.

"I'm sorry." She continued, and Bea genuinely had no idea what she was apologizing for.

"For what?" she asked.

"For not being more patient with you. I had time, those couple days, to acclimate. And you didn't get that, I should have realized you'd need to adjust too."

"Oh."

It was so sweet, and soft, and sincere—that gentle side of Evian that Bea craved to see more of. She could almost feel the comfort of Evian's fingers running through her hair again. The ghost in the kitchen, or hallucination—or whatever it was—began to fade.

"I really am sorry I snapped at you. I think I just have been wanting to use you as a distraction? I know that's selfish, and I didn't realize that's what I was doing. It's only that I like spending this time with you more than I like thinking about what happened."

Bea's sister was gone. Gone from the world. Her after-image was gone from the kitchen too. The room felt brighter and there was a nagging feeling that a life here with Evian opening up like this couldn't possibly be so bad.

She almost believed it, too. That there was nothing supernatural going on, and that all the oddities had been nothing more than shock. There were no guidebooks about how to feel when the world ended. Her mind was just trying to come to terms with an unfathomable loss. Right?

But still, her heart told her to fight it.

"I'm sorry I pushed you to talk about it. But the time dealing with it myself is helping."

"I understand that now. If there's anything I can do to help you with it today, I'll do it."

Her chance.

On a silver platter, Evian was offering her the chance she needed to test the limits of her impact on the house.

"I would take another book, if you happen to have one lying around."

"Of course," Evian answered. She seemed too happy about it. "Let me see what I can find for you."

It didn't take her more than a minute to return with a small stack of bestsellers that she brought back from the void somewhere. "Is that all you need?"

Bea smiled. "Is it okay if I have some time alone on the couch to read them? Another day of quiet should really calm my nerves."

"Of course. But Bea?" Evian offered her the books.

"Yes?"

"Would you mind coming back to bed tonight? To our bed?"

The words shook something in her core. That they shared a bed. That Evian could have a full night to tempt her, to distract her from the answers she sought. By morning she would be too wrapped up to even care about all the things they'd left behind and lost for good.

"Tonight." She confirmed as she took the books. She agreed because it had not been a request, but a bargain. On some level she understood that. She and Evian may have all the time in the world, but she only had the one day left to learn what she needed.

12.

Evian took her sweet time getting ready to leave, but there was no sign she was doing it to frustrate Bea. She looked at ease when she did finally cross through the living room again to the front door in her two-piece. Bea made a show of looking over the books, flipping through them and studying the back covers from the comfort of the couch. Not a single word stuck.

"I'll see you for dinner?" Evian asked.

Bea made it a point not to look up from the book. "Sure thing."

It must have worked, because it was a carefree Evian who didn't look back at her once after stepping past the threshold. Bea waited with held breath for as long as she could bear it before setting down the novel.

She raced to the hall.

There were many things she expected to happen when she tried the big door at the end of it. She prepared herself for the worst, an alarm to go off, a trap to be triggered—she even considered that as soon as she tried to force her way inside Evian might just appear behind her with a knife. Expectations have a way of running wild for those who cannot differentiate between nightmares and reality.

But nothing happened when she touched the door where it waited for her. The other doors were all shiny, lacquered wood with brassy handles. This one was frosted glass in a steel frame, so thick and clouded that it would have blended right into the white walls were it not outlined in silver.

She grabbed the handle and pulled.

She gasped.

The one thing she had not been prepared for was for the door to yield to her on the first try. Stepping into the room, she almost wished it hadn't.

It was colorless on that side of the door. The walls, floor, and ceiling were all spotted in a black-and-white pattern that her brain interpreted as a hazy gray upon first notice. Looking a bit more carefully, it appeared more like TV static, and she could swear it was moving.

The whole area swallowed any point of reference or sense of space to the point it seemed amorphous, and she struggled to think of it as a room when it felt more like a void.

It was vacuous, but not empty.

Lying haphazardly on the floor she could see an assortment of items—her laptop, Evian's tablet, an old music player from the bottom of her purse, two phones. Her eyes landed on a smashed and broken clock, which she recognized from the living room where it had hung on their arrival.

Bea knew she was standing in a sort of junk closet then, albeit the most elaborate junk closet she had ever seen. It was filled with the things Evian had wanted to hide from her.

She moved to her phone first.

It felt heavier in her hand than she expected it to, more real than so many of the objects she'd been interacting with. The moment she touched it, she felt grounded once more to reality—as she'd felt putting on the jeans.

That was what it felt like, she reckoned, to touch things that were real.

She tapped at the home button and almost dropped it when it lit up. She'd expected it to be dead and remain black; not to show her a picture of Evian.

The picture of Evian.

The memories came flooding back to her all at once, pent up from a full week of absence. Vivid recollections streamed into her mind—of all the nights she had fallen asleep, staring at that exact picture, fantasizing about its subject. It was the picture she thought of on her bad days, the picture she had tried to manifest for herself, the end goal that had inspired years of her life. Her studies. Her move from home. Her fights with her mother. Her interviews. They had all started with one viral photo of the woman she had loved at first sight.

That made her situation feel all the more impossible. She had loved this woman from afar for so long, and had been forced to fight to even get to a point where they could be in the same room together.

Alone on an island with the woman of her dreams, it was hardly any wonder she'd been suspicious of the experience. It rang far too good to be true.

But she had worked for it. She'd fought. And now that she was there, she couldn't believe how hard she had been trying to sabotage the opportunity. Was a life with Evian something she was willing to throw away for the sake of her sanity?

The guilt gnawed at her for her lack of gratitude. She felt that if she were a smarter, more generous person, she would turn around and lock up this forbidden room with its memories. She knew it would be better for her, and for her love, if she turned away and tried to forget all that she had seen.

It would be so easy.

If she wanted to, she could go and join Evian on the beach, and they could eat dinner and go to bed, and pretend that everything was okay. They could live out the rest of their lives in a perfect fantasy as they had tried to do that first night.

But her curiosity was a burning scar in her gut. It was the itch of rough skin.

She unlocked her phone screen. The first thing she noticed when Evian's face was no longer staring at her was the time.

11:49 p.m.

The second thing she noticed was the battery, which told her it was at thirty-two percent. It could not have been any higher than that when she slipped it into her jacket pocket to be stolen away from her. Yet she also doubted anyone had come into this room to charge it before abandoning it to the floor.

She felt frozen in that little pocket of 11:49 p.m., where things did not—or could not—change.

She went through the pictures in her phone reel next, scrolling through the snapshots from her last several months of life. Many of those memories set to record were, of course, of Evian. Behind-the-scenes content for the socials, yes, but also stolen glimpses into what it would be like if the two were alone. Fodder for her fantasies of what it might be like to live together.

The photos did not span far enough back to encapsulate her time—the majority of her life, really—spent living out east. It did not even have her depressed college days, which had been spent coping after the worst thing imaginable had happened to her family.

Not to her, but to her sister.

Elle.

The name came back to her with such force that she almost cried out.

Elle.

How could she have forgotten? Why were all her memories of the world before only available to her in this one room? Where had they been before when she had needed to grieve, and mourn, and feel bad over her own selfish actions?

Scrolling through the camera roll and her saved pictures desperately, she realized it was not just the island. Even before the end, she had worked hard to forget what had happened between them. Her sister's name stopped coming up in her day-to-day conversations. Their already-infrequent calls died out altogether. Bea hadn't wanted to think about her failure.

She'd been relieved.

When she had gotten the news that the world was ending, she had been so glad.

So why had she, of all people, been allowed to keep on going?

There were no additional pictures of her sister or mother, or any ties to who she had been before things had gone to hell. Social media links weren't working. Frantically, she pulled up her messages.

The last message she'd ever sent—Surprise, surprise—

had been to Evian. It read simply: "See you soon."

She scrolled up in that conversation thread to see a brief exchange about when and where they'd meet, a couple questions about what she needed to bring. Everything above that was all business.

She searched for the last messages she'd sent to her mother, to Elle, but they were so far down. Something inside her broke when she saw the last message she'd ever sent to her mother: "Ask Elle."

Reading that, she could remember the conversation all too well. Elle had gone back home, back east, and she hadn't been sleeping or eating or taking care of herself. She had quit caring about her friends and her looks, and her grades. She'd almost flunked out her senior year.

Everyone knew that something had happened. That she had changed.

But it was the thing they didn't talk about, and Bea hadn't wanted to be the one to break the silence. Elle had told her not to, and it wasn't Bea's story to tell. So she'd had to live with the guilt, and bury a thing she'd rather have confronted. And it had changed her. It had built a chasm.

"Ask Elle." She had told her mother when the calls and the messages hadn't stopped. "Ask Elle. Ask Elle. Ask Elle."

Her mother had probably tried that, had probably started with that solution and tried time and again before giving up. Then she gave up on Bea too.

And what had Bea had to turn to, except to her pic-ture-perfect life working for Evian? The lavish lifestyle that had been so alluring, and which had burned her sister on the first taste.

She pressed the "Call" button.

"Mom, you were right," she wanted to say. "You were right about everything. I should never have moved away. I should have taken better care of Elle when she came to visit. She got hurt and it was my fault, and I was too scared to tell you. Now everything's over, and I've gotten myself into some real trouble. I miss you, Mom. And I don't know what I'm doing. I don't know how to make it right. I'm scared."

But she didn't say that.

Her mother didn't answer.

Her mother was dead, just like her sister, just like ev-eryone else in the world. It was just as Evian had said.

There was no one else.

Even if Bea would gladly give up her position on the island to her more deserving family, it was too late to think of all that now. Maybe distraction was all that could be hoped for, in lack of the chance to undo her mess.

She set her phone back down on the ground, too emp-ty to even cry.

When she stepped back into the hall, she wasn't sur-prised to find Evian waiting for her. She was surprised to see the tears in her lover's eyes, as if she had been the one in the static room, dealing with years of unpacked trauma. When their gazes locked, Bea realized with horror that she had seen that expression on Evian's face before.

"Bea, we talked about this."

"Did we?"

They had, very briefly, over pasta. That memory was clearer now, too, and she knew it had not ended well.

"I don't understand why you can't just be happy with me."

Bea didn't understand either. Not really, and especially not now that she had felt the horrid pain of facing her reality. Still. "It's just not easy to pretend that I don't know."

"You're the one making it difficult."

"You said I could have today."

"You said you'd be reading."

It's true. She had mentioned reading. She had asked for books. She hadn't wanted Evian to know what she was doing, because she was sure Evian wouldn't want to let her do it.

"I'm sorry." She tried to step back into that room, which was no real room at all, but she couldn't find the handle with her back pressed against the door. Evian advanced on her. "I'm sorry," she said again, her voice strained and weak.

"Me too." Evian told her.

She cupped Bea's face in her hands, and Bea found the tears that had, just a minute before, evaded her.

"Don't be angry with me," she pleaded. "I just wanted

to understand what was going on. I wanted to remember how we got here."

"I know," Evian whispered. "I know you didn't mean to hurt me. But I can't have you going around poking holes in everything."

Thunder shook the island.

"Poking holes?"

Instead of an answer, Evian's fingers closed around her head in a vice grip. Bea barely had time to panic before her lover twisted. Hard.

The last thing she heard was the snapping of her own neck.

Part 3

13.

The orange light that had swallowed the sky was gone, replaced with many small, flickering lights in the shape of lit torches, fighting back the dark. For a moment, Bea almost believed that the world ending had been nothing but a terrible dream.

Either way, she woke from it, and into an absolute nightmare.

When her vision cleared enough, and her head stopped pounding, she struggled to take a look around and make what sense she could of her predicament. It was like staring back through time as her eyes focused on the stone wall in front of her. It was cold, rustic, and lit only with the torches.

"This can't be happening."

Her cracked voice was weak, and further muffled by

the oppressive damp of the dungeon.

Dungeon.

The word sank in, and she panicked. She tried to pull herself from the floor to make a run for it, only to be tugged back to the wall by her wrists, which had gone numb while she slept. She whipped her around. The motion elicited a sharp stab of pain through her bruised neck, and it ran bone deep, all the way through her spine.

When the sensation subsided enough, there were no longer spots of white in her vision, she was able to see a heavy iron ring embedded in the wall just above her head. A short chain ran through it, encircling her at the wrists. She tugged against such restraints violently and was rewarded only with a cacophonous clinking that set her head to pounding again. She could maneuver the chain left or right a little, stretching one arm up to give the other some slack, but it was uncomfortable and painful. For all intents and purposes, her arms were stuck.

She was stuck.

"This can't be happening."

She slumped back against the wall and watched the torches flicker. She had a little bit of time to put things into perspective. The memory of the world's end reminded her that being held captive in a medieval dungeon was not the worst thing that had happened lately. There was a sore spot of a scar on her stomach, and the fresh pain in her neck that suggested it was not even the worst thing that had happened to her lately.

All the same, Bea couldn't weather another shift in her reality. A human mind could only handle so much, and hers was already on the verge of cracking open. She was losing touch with what was and was not real.

When she heard a door opening from somewhere above her, she found herself more relieved than she had any right to be.

"Evian?" she called. "Evian, please help!"

She only noticed the dark stairs once she saw the figure descending them. Her heart swelled to see that it was indeed Evian, who looked calm and unbothered. "Oh good, you're awake."

Bea babbled through her tears. "Evian, please help me. You have to let me out. I don't know how I got down here or where the key is but…"

She trailed off into silence when she saw Evian was holding an ornate iron key. "You mean this?"

"Please…" She tried to swallow, but her mouth was too dry to give any relief to her throat. "Let me out."

Evian tucked the key into the back pocket of her skin-tight jeans before kneeling down in front of Bea, cupping her cheek. "I wish I could."

"You can. Please? Evian, I'm so scared."

"I know, pet. I know."

Pet.

She couldn't help but recall how such a name had thrilled her the last time she'd been bound at Evian's mercy.

"This isn't a game." She sobbed. "This isn't okay." She shook her head weakly and had to stop even that small sign of resistance for the throbbing that followed. "You need to let me out."

Evian's thumb stroked Bea's cheek in a slow, gentle movement. She tried to recoil, but there was nowhere to go, and every small motion hurt her further.

"It's not a game, no." Her voice dripped with sympathy that bordered on condescending. It made Bea as angry as she was scared.

"What the fuck, Evian?"

"Will you give me the chance to explain?"

A small voice of rationality told her that she should, that her best chance of escape was to play docile. In her current state, such a performance should not have been difficult, but she found she was too angry and too tired of hiding her accusations.

"Explain what? You fucking... You snapped my neck and dragged me down here and chained my up against my will."

Evian pulled away, giving a sad smile that made Bea want to slap her. "Bea, love, do you hear how that sounds?"

"It's what happened," she growled. "I remember it."

"Do you?"

"Yes!"

"Then tell me. Tell me what exactly it is you think you remember."

"You broke my neck. You dragged me down here. You chained me up."

"How did I break your neck, Bea?"

They had been in the hallway. They'd been fighting. The memories themselves were liquid, but the impressions of them left tall shadows in her mind. "We were in the hall. You attacked me again."

Evian shook her head, flaunting another freedom Bea didn't have. "I never attacked you."

"The fuck you didn't! I have the scars to prove it. Evian, I'm not messing around. I'm freaking out and you need to unlock me right now. I'm not kidding."

"Bea, you freaking out is the reason you need to stay there."

"You don't get to decide that!"

"I need you to listen to me. You hurt yourself."

"I broke my own neck?" she asked, incredulous.

"You pulled a muscle in your own neck." Evian corrected. "You could have done some real damage thrashing around the way you were. I think you were having another episode."

"Episode?" She shrieked so loud that she could feel the

vibrations in her coarse throat.

"Yes, episode. Like when you tried to gut yourself with a dinner knife."

"When you stabbed me, you mean."

"Bea, I would never hurt you."

"I have the scar."

"You gave it to yourself."

She felt hysterical. She wanted to laugh. Or cry. Maybe both. All she could do was squeeze her eyes shut and try to hold onto what she knew was true. "I didn't hurt myself."

"But you did, pet. Twice now."

There was that word again. Pet.

She opened her eyes, and spoke calmly as she held Evian's gaze. "Evian, you do not have my consent to do this. What you've done here is a violation of my boundaries and you have to unlock me right now."

"It's like you said, Bea. This isn't a game. I know that you're into this sort of thing." She tugged on one of the chains, an action that sent a wave of pain through Bea's whole body. "But this is strictly for your own protection until I can figure something out."

Gone was her resolve to stay calm no matter what. "I'm into this sort of thing?" She demanded. "You have a fucking dungeon in the basement of your vacation home—don't you dare pretend that you've done this for me."

The staged look of concern on the blonde's face faltered in her amusement. There was still the ghost of a smirk on her lips as she spoke. "I never said I didn't like it, too. But you're the one who begged for me to tie you to our bed, remember?"

"Now I'm begging you to untie me."

"I would, Bea, if I thought you could be trusted."

She felt insane. She felt absolutely insane. "If I could be trusted?"

Evian stroked her hair. "I won't do anything to you if you don't want it. This doesn't have to be one of our games, since you don't seem to be in the mood. But I hope you understand, I can't have you running around hurting yourself. I think maybe it's for the best if you stay down here until you've had the chance to calm down. Then we can decide together how to handle this."

"Don't touch me," she snapped.

Evian pulled her hand away, compliant. It gave her just the tiniest spark of false hope.

"Let me go."

"You know I can't do that."

"Can't? Or won't?"

Evian sighed. "What sort of person would I be if I didn't take care of you?"

Bea couldn't help but laugh. "Is this how you take care of someone?"

"When they're being unreasonable."

"I wish you had died," she snapped. "I wish we had both died with the rest of the world."

The color drained from Evian's face in a way that didn't seem entirely for show. "Do you see what I mean, Bea?"

"About what?"

"You need help. You believe that the world ended."

14.

The biggest difference between her waking and dreaming worlds was the pain. Bea's thoughts were clearer when she slept, and when she woke the aches and pains of captivity kept her more present in her physical torment.

Her shoulders screamed in protest at being kept in an unnatural position for so long. Her jaw ached from the gag Evian had wedged between her teeth—afraid after the second or third day that Bea's constant screams would open up another tear in the world through which more static may leak in.

She could reposition a little, which took the pressure off her knees, but doing so tugged at her chafed wrists and woke the muscles of her back up enough to truly burn. Her hair grew greasy and tangled from all her futile attempts to get free. The front of her shirt grew soaked from the drool that was constantly escaping from around the edges of her gag. She had long since stopped the losing battle of sucking the saliva back into her mouth, which she could no longer close properly.

She didn't have any true way to tell how long she'd been kept in the basement. Her phone had been stashed away again, along with the clock and the clarity of her memories. The torches on the wall never went out or dwindled, and she did not even have a window to track the changing colors of the post-apocalyptic sky that Evian swore up and down was still as blue and bright as ever. It was one reason why Bea had been screaming, to tune out all such lies.

Such stagnation as hers could easily have been maddening, but luckily Bea knew exactly what time it was.

It was 11:49 for now and always.

If she could see the sky, she could have proof that it had all been true, but Evian would not let that happen. Seeing through the illusion made it fragile and until Bea could be broken, she would be a threat.

She didn't know how she knew, but the logic of dreams persisted. Her dreams were, if anything, more real than reality most days that she was locked away.

15.

"Will you please have some water?"

The first time Evian had come down to undo the buckle of the gag and let her work out her stiff jaw, Bea had been so grateful. She'd been eager to take the food and drink offered, and started the interaction desperate to get back on Evian's good side.

Then they had fought anyway. Bea didn't have it in her to pretend that the unimaginable wasn't happening. She couldn't lie convincingly to say she believed the sky would be nice and normal when they made it upstairs together. She couldn't act like the world had not ended.

So they had argued, which had turned into screaming, and the gag had been put back in her mouth, and she'd been left alone for another eternity. Things went still again, and the isolation felt even worse than before because she had lost all hope.

So this time, when Evian returned, she stayed silent, and went so far as to turn her head away from the water bottle when it was brought up to her lips.

Mind over matter.

That was a skill she'd had plenty of time to hone in the countless hours she'd spent alone in the dungeon. Her mental abilities were becoming more important to her than any lessening of her physical discomfort.

The trick, she'd learned, was not to expect herself to hurt.

Expectations and perception had more sway on reality here than she had previously realized. Bea didn't have as strong a hold on the world's shape as Evian seemed to, but she had figured out the game enough that she could no longer be manipulated by something as simple as the promise of water. She could not do much to free herself, but she could at the very least not hand over and more control to Evian.

"Bea, please." Evian begged.

Bea shook her head.

Her mouth was too dry for her to even attempt speaking. She wasn't drooling anymore, that's how bad it had gotten. The last of her body's moisture was slowly drying from the sticky T-shirt fabric covering her breasts.

"You need to drink."

The concern sounded real, but lacked substance. What

she needed was not to drink, and they both knew it.

"I'm getting really worried about you."

Bea had plenty of thoughts about that, but she kept them to herself. Her mental energy was valuable, and not to be wasted. When Evian pried her mouth open and almost drowned her by shoving the water down her parched throat, she didn't fight it too hard. Not because it offered solace, but because trying something she might fail would make her lose more ground than her choice to concede up front.

"I brought you food, too."

No response.

"You need to eat."

Bea didn't care.

"Please don't make me force-feed you."

Bea didn't doubt that Evian would force-feed her, either, if it came down to it. She imagined being choked on thick tubes forced down her throat, blended shakes being poured into her stomach without giving her a chance to taste. It couldn't be more uncomfortable than all she'd been through already—and part of her thought it might be worth it just for the trouble it would make for Evian. But she turned her mind from the thought. To picture it could be to make it so, and such a predicament was not productive to her point.

At last, she spoke.

"Are you worried I'll die?" She didn't recognize the voice that came crackling from between her lips; the dry static sound of something about to burn.

"Yes," Evian replied softly.

"Does it matter that I'm already dead?"

The relief on her lover's face dried up. "Stop that."

"I died, Evian."

"No."

"You killed me."

"You know I can't stand to see you like this."

"And you killed me once before that, too."

"Stop."

"And I think once before that, we died together."

"Stop it!" Evian shrieked, recoiling.

The world lost some of its color.

Bea smiled, even as she saw Evian reaching for the gag again. "I'm right, aren't I? It's why you can't stand to listen to this."

"I can't stand to listen to this because you're having a psychotic break and I'm worried about you."

Evian was a good actress, but Bea had planned for this. She had the mental ammunition ready. If the world was fine, and the two lovers were just on vacation, and Bea was having a mental break, help would have arrived for her already. She would be getting treatment. She wouldn't be locked in a basement. She didn't think even Evian could conjure other people to this strange place where the pair found themselves.

She knew better than to point it out, though.

Logic could only get her so far, and saying such things only gave Evian a chance to refute them, to come up with more lies, to sow more uncertainty in her already-stretched capacity for understanding.

"Why are you afraid of me not eating?" she asked instead.

"Because you'll die, Bea."

"I think you're more afraid that I won't die."

"No."

"If you leave me down here to rot, and I don't, you'll have to face the truth, Evian."

"Bea, please. Listen to yourself."

"How many eggs are in the fridge?"

"Stop it."

"What time is it right now?"

The room was thrumming and gray as her point was made.

Evian slapped her so hard across the face that her left ear rang in pain. The static stopped. The color returned. The illusion grew stronger as Bea fed it with her sensory connection. "This is why I locked you down here!" Evian snarled.

But even that admission was a sign that Bea had done it. She had proven her point. She had won.

Somehow, Bea had won. Evian had broken first.

"Why can't you just be honest?" she asked, the taste of her blood in her mouth, the gag forgotten. Evian was staring at the imprint of her hand in horror.

"Because we don't have to be," she answered.

"Yes, we do."

"No, Bea. We don't. It's just the two of us here. And we are here. We can just keep going and going. We can make each other breakfast and lie out on the beach and swim and just live. We can make love. I can take care of you, like I promised."

"Evian, you have to see that this isn't real. None of this is real."

"Stop saying that. It's only true if you say it. If you would just stop, and let me do this, I could make all your wildest fantasies come true and we can live in them for the rest of our lives."

"Our lives are over, Evian."

"Why don't you want this?"

"We had one fling—"

"Stop."

"—and now it's over."

"But it doesn't have to be!" There was a wild, dangerous look in Evian's eyes. "I can keep this going forever if you stop fighting me. This place is nothing more than what we make of it, and all I want is for that to be something good."

Bea wished she could believe that as wholeheartedly as Evian did. When she looked back, all the best parts of their situation had been created by Evian, who wanted something better for them. All the fear and pain and panic had been caused by her trying to understand, and from that perspective she was the enemy here. She was a danger that needed to be locked away until she succumbed. If she'd stop looking for the horrors, and asking questions, maybe they really could just have it all, in whatever bliss Evian could think to create.

But Bea didn't think so.

"I think this place wouldn't exist if we were honest with ourselves about what we're doing here."

"Then let's lie together."

"I can't keep lying, Evian. I did that before…and it made me a different person. I died with regrets, and I don't want to carry them anymore."

"Then don't. Let them go. Let me bury them."

"Do you have regrets, too?"

"No," Evian said. "I don't regret anything that brought me here."

"Do you think maybe there's a chance," Bea asked gently, "that you're holding onto this all so tightly because you feel guilty?"

"Guilty about what?"

There was a time in Bea's life where she never would have thought to blame Evian for a single thing. Not Evian, who was beautiful, and perfect, and unobtainable. But they were too far past that. Chained and tired and nearly beaten, she felt braver in admitting that maybe not all of her notions about her lover were true.

"I think you regret not being with me when we had the chance to do it right."

"What?"

"You were always so worried about your image that you never wanted to be seen with me. Not until the very end. And you liked it, and now you feel bad that you didn't risk it all sooner."

"That's not true, Bea."

"But it is. I was too fat, or too poor. And I always idolized you, and you saw me as nothing but an obsessed fan with a crush, who wouldn't look good standing in any of your pictures or going to your fancy parties."

"I never thought that." Bea would have been moved by how hurt Evian looked at the implication, if she weren't so hopeful about gaining more ground.

"But you did. Somewhere deep down you did, because the only place you ever found for me in your life was behind the screen editing your photos."

"You worked for me. That was your job." The room around them paled and faded as Evian's focus turned to rationalization.

"And we both wanted more! I can be honest about my regrets, why can't you be honest about yours?"

Evian locked eyes with her, her expression pleading. "We don't have to have regrets. We have all the time in the world now."

"I wish," Bea started, and immediately faltered. The words were harder to find than she had hoped. Years of striving to please this woman had her ready to crumble under such a gaze. She persevered, only with the knowledge that if she did not continue now, she would never find the strength again. "I wish you would be honest with me, about why you're holding on so tight."

"I am being honest, Bea." And in her own sick way, she was. Maybe more honest than she had ever been. Bea could see that now, a rare vulnerability from someone who was used to being strong. "I don't want this to end. I don't want to lose you."

"You don't have me. This isn't me. The longer we're here the harder it is for me to remember things."

"Things that have the potential to ruin everything we've built! Lose them. You don't need those things."

Bea straightened up; the protest of her aching muscles weak in comparison to her hurt over the implication. "Are you so afraid of being alone that you don't even care I'm losing myself? Would you rather drive me to insanity and keep me chained in the basement than admit I'm right?"

"Do you think I want to keep you suffering like this?" Evian snapped. "If you just promise me that you'll stop poking around and ruining this and asking questions, I'll let you out. We can go upstairs, and we can just live the life we never had together. We can make the most of whatever this is. Promise me."

"I can't promise you that."

"It's all I want."

"I know. But it's not real, Evian, and I can't live the lie. I don't want to lose the memories I have left."

"We'll make new memories."

"They won't be real." Bea could feel the tears burning behind her eyes. "None of this is real."

Evian stood up and shook her head. "No. You're going to come around. You're going to learn to see it my way, and stop fighting, and you're going to be so glad I did this for you."

"Evian…"

"I'll let you out when you're ready to live in paradise with me. When you're ready to accept that I can make this all better."

Evian left her again.

She never did replace the gag, but neither did she push the bowl of food within reach.

16.

Bea used to play The Desert Island Game with her sister, Elle. They would sit in the tiny bedroom they shared, and spend hours making their respective lists of five things that they could bring to keep them company if they were stranded on a fictional desert island.

Movies.
Books.
TV shows.
Albums.
Games.

They'd write their lists on notebook paper and fold them up like the secret notes that would be passed around in a classroom. When they had both finished, they'd exchange folded squares of paper, giggling, their arms sticking out from the sides of their bunk bed and blindly reaching for each other.

As they'd gotten older, there had been less and less crossover between lists. They'd been as good as strangers as they had grown, they were so different.

Elle had gotten pretty, and popular, and she'd had neither the time nor interest to waste away passing notes to her pathetic big sister in a house she so resented.

Bea's life had, for the most part, gone quiet.

Their mother would be out, working. Elle would be doing her extracurricular activities, or sleeping over at someone's house. Bea would be left home alone more often than not. Even though she was older, and in theory wiser, she had always leaned more heavily on the escapism that their little game had offered. She kept playing it alone, through most of her school years.

It was a challenge for her, always, to pick only five of everything. How could a person choose only five worlds to live in amongst the countless offered in the library?

Five moods offered from the entire range of music?

The digital age had made the game feel all the more hypothetical, almost obsolete.

If she were stranded somewhere at any given time, she would be with her phone or laptop or the old music player that she'd received second-hand as a gift for graduating middle school with honors, and had never stopped carrying. She'd have whole catalogues, discographies, endless entertainment at her fingertips.

Yet she always wanted to keep putting them into lists. Countless hours she had spent hyper-focused on such a thing, only for the hypothetical to come true and for it not to matter.

Stranded as she was, it was with all her favorite media digitally preserved on the floor above her. She'd found her desert island, and someone—an impossible beauty—to share it with, and even though the whole arrangement ran on the same imagination that had gotten her through the roughest times in her life, she couldn't make it work.

She had not chosen escapism.

She'd chosen to focus on the bad.

She'd chosen a dungeon over the love of her life, and with each passing day she spent alone, it grew harder to remember why.

For guilt?

For memories of a sister who had long since abandoned her?

In the hours she spent waiting for Evian to return to her, she tried to remember what had happened to Elle—what terrible thing had happened that had been the final nail in the coffin of their relationship. What trauma had she been running from?

She could never conjure those answers when she was awake, and trying to, but sometimes she got glimpses of such a past while she slept.

Her coming out.

Her moving out.

College.

Elle visiting her for her birthday.

A bar.

A man.

Bea had been sick in the bathroom of the dorm, and Elle had been laughing in her bed with a man. But she couldn't remember what had happened after that, what it was that had sent her little sister home broken.

Then again, she couldn't remember most things when she was awake. All her memories were held captive with her media, a floor above her, locked away in a room that was made of static.

She would have played The Desert Island game for comfort if she could have, but the media that had raised her, formed her, strengthened her even, reached her mind as little more than echoes too fluid to order into a list.

She wondered if she would have a better grasp on her sense of self if she could remember five books or movies or albums that had kept her going in her darkest hours when she'd needed them before. But she didn't have that any longer. She was alone. Abandoned.

She slept and woke and wondered, her mind often going blank and colorless to tune into the static that lingered

just behind the illusion of the island prison.
    The torches never went out.
    The fruit in the bowl never rotted.
    A long time passed where nothing changed.

17.

"Are you feeling better?"

"I am."

"You look better."

"Thanks."

"Did you think about what I said?"

"I did."

"And? Are you ready to come upstairs with me?"

Bea looked up at Evian. She was still as beautiful as ever, and had dressed up for the occasion. She wore a seafoam sundress that brought out the green in her eyes—even in the erratic orange lighting of the dungeon. She looked far too delicate to be in a place like this.

Bea was still covered in filth, the sweat and blood and drool of her imprisonment coating her from head to toe. On some level she knew it was silly to feel self-conscious about the condition another person had inflicted upon her, but she couldn't stop the tickling of old insecurities.

What choice did she have, though? She was only going to get worse until she got out of there.

"I am."

Evian toyed with the key that hung around her neck, where she wore Bea's freedom like expensive jewelry. "You aren't going to make a run for it, are you?"

"No." Bea told her.

"You aren't going to hurt yourself again?"

So that was the game they were playing. Back to denial. Even that had to be better than where she sat.

"No," Bea answered.

"Promise me." Evian commanded.

"I promise."

Evian kept looking at her, expectant.

"I promise, I'm done." She confirmed. "I'm just so tired, Evian. I'm ready to give up."

Evian must have known she meant it, because she knelt down and, at long last, unlocked the manacles. Bea's arms fell like leaden weights to her sides. Her body slumped forward, and Evian had to catch her.

"I'll ruin your dress." She protested.

"That doesn't matter."

Evian helped pull her to her feet and guide her up the

stairs on her shaky legs. She was not as malnourished or dehydrated as she ought to have been, but every part of her ached.

They came up into the house through a door that Bea was certain hadn't been there before, but that was of little consequence in comparison to the blinding light. Even with the shutters drawn and the overheads on at their dimmest setting, she had to squint so as not to be overwhelmed. Evian led her to the bathtub and stripped away her soiled clothes.

She turned the shower onto Bea and scrubbed her affectionately to remove the top layer of grime.

Bea just curled up in the bottom of the tub and let her work.

When the worst of it was done, Evian put the stopper into the tub and coated the porcelain with a sweet layer of scented bubbles. She leaned Bea back into the warm concoction.

"We're never going to have to go through anything like that again, okay?"

"Okay."

"Can I bring you anything?"

"Water?" she asked, her voice still weak. "One of the sparkling ones?"

"Of course."

Evian bent down first to plant a kiss on her forehead, and Bea sprang into action before she'd made up her mind to do it. The razor was in her hand, slashing across Evian's neck before she had time to reconsider.

She wasn't even sure where she had gotten it from, whether it had been at the edge of the tub, or if she had simply willed it into her hand like so many books.

At first, she was convinced she hadn't gone deep enough, as Evian froze in place with wide eyes. Then, Bea watched in slow motion as the red line opened up in her lover's neck. Evian's mouth opened, but the blood burbling from her throat caught whatever words she tried to utter. She brought her hands up to stop the stream, but it only tore wider, and she fell back onto the floor.

Bea got out of the tub and pulled Evian into her arms, stroking her hair to calm the spluttering, wheezing sounds.

"Shhh," she whispered. "You're okay."

Evian's red-splattered nails clawed at her throat, and Bea just rocked her back and forth, with a gentle, soothing, "Shhh."

She let a little time pass before she spoke again, collecting her thoughts. Deciding how it would be.

"You're going to wake up from this, and we're going to talk about it. And whatever happens next…we'll face it together, okay?"

The panic in her eyes faded to glassy, colorless static, and her body went limp.

"It's okay." Bea told her. "You're going to be okay."

She cleaned up as much of the blood from herself and

Evian as she could before dragging the body into the master bedroom. Only then did she take a few minutes for an extra shower.

As she scrubbed the blood from her skin, a terrible thought crossed her mind.

What if Evian doesn't wake up?

But she would.

Of course she would. She had to.

Bea had died three times that she knew of since their arrival to the island, and Evian was so much stronger than her. She'd pull through, and when she did, they could talk about the power imbalance and the guilt and how to move past it. She just had to have faith that Evian would wake again and come to find her underneath the orange sky to talk about the world ending.

She'd done it once before, after all.

By the time Bea dried off and changed into clean clothes, she could hear the storm brewing overhead. She didn't know if that was a good or bad sign, but the thunder was enough to shake their little island once again.

She drank two full bottles of the sparkling water which she left on the counter in the hopes the mess would clean itself. As the house stayed quiet around her, Bea began to doubt her actions. She began to doubt herself.

There was just one thing that she needed to check, even if it was silly. She knew it could put her mind at ease while she waited for Evian.

She poked her head outside the front door, hoping to quell her fears with a peak at a blood-red sky. Only that's not what waited for her. The sky was not red, nor was it its normal blue as part of her had feared. It was charcoal gray, and raining down a static that dissolved the trees around her into a void.

18.

Bea stretched her body out in the cool sand, storm be damned.

She had plenty of regrets as she let herself get soaked through, the scent of the salt fading as surely as the color of the world. There were so many things she wished she could have experienced before it was over, things she would have explored more thoroughly the mysteries which she still longed to understand.

Bea hoped Evian would wake up in time for her to apologize. Then they could watch everything they'd built together sink into oblivion.

She seemed to recall she'd had the best sex of her life the first time the world had ended, and wouldn't mind going for a second round, just in case it was really over.

Acknowledgments

There are so many people I'd like to thank for making this book possible. First and foremost, Wayne Fenlon, who created the gorgeous cover that inspired the piece. Then there are all the lovely beta-readers and critique partners who supported me in this project.

I want to give a special thanks to David-Jack and Lee for taking a chance on my weird little story and helping me get it polished up and out into the universe. For better or worse.

Finally, I'd like to thank you, the person reading this. Thanks for going on a trip to the end of the world with me.

About the Author

Cat Voleur is a full-time horror journalist, and co-founder of The Sinister Scoop. She is a cohost of Slasher Radio and The Nic F'n Woo Cage Cast. She lives with a small army of rescue felines who encourage her to create and consume morbid content. In her free time, you can most likely find her pursuing her passion for fictional languages.

Website: catvoleur.com